errigal

SEARCH FOR THE BLUE STONE

Published 2011

Cover design and illustrations: Jim Lavery • www.jimlaveryart.com

Publisher: Little Acorn Press, N. Ireland.
email: littleacornpress@gmail.com

Editor: Ruth Carr

British Library Cataloguing in Publication Data
A CIP catalogue record for this book is available from the British Library.

ISBN: 978-0-9568900-0-9

Printed in the UK by W&G Baird, Greystone Road, Antrim, BT41 2RS.
All Ireland Printers since 1862.

For details on how to order additional copies of this book please visit:

www.errigalthebook.com

Acknowledgments

I would like to thank Emma, Hannah and Michael for inspiring me to write this story.

Thanks also to my nieces Katie, Megan, Lucy, Amy and Elaine and my nephews Danny, Luke, Caleb, Adam, Jack and Alexander. The encouragement you gave me by listening to my stories over the years is one of the reasons I eventually put pen to paper.

Thanks to Mum and Dad for all those wonderful holidays in Donegal where I first saw and climbed Errigal.

Thanks to the brilliant artwork from Jim Lavery and for his help in getting the book ready for printing.

Thanks to Scott Thompson for designing the website. I am very grateful to Ruth Carr for the editing and good advice she provided.

Also thank you to the team at W&G Baird for the print work.

Finally, thank you to my husband Trevor who first put the idea of writing a story into my head and never gave up on me.

For Emma, Hannah and Michael.

Chapter 1

As she turned the corner at the top of the street, Mel found a group of threatening faces staring at her. This gave her a tough decision to make. On the one hand she could abruptly turn in her tracks and run like the wind back down to her safe little haven, better known as home. Or, in an act of defiance, she could continue down the street, ignoring the intimidating stares and smirks of the others and quite simply proceed with what she had set out to do... to go to Gallagher's to stock up with her weekly supply of sweets.

However, more often than not she got it wrong. You see, although being accepted by the crowd was one of her greatest desires, Mel was hot-headed and stubborn. Her approach to Gallagher's usually concluded with snide remarks from the local kids referring to her quirky style and her 'I'm better than you' manner.

What they didn't realise was that this was exactly how Mel dealt with being an outcast. By holding her head up and looking the other way, she managed to convey a clear message of 'What do I care?'

If you continued past Gallagher's, you would come to a junction. A left turn would lead you down a gravelly lane onto the beach. Nothing very special about this beach, except that it had one outstanding landmark, an old fishing boat sitting at an odd angle on the sand. It should have been removed years ago to create more space for holiday makers. The general consensus among the locals, however, was that it was a good talking point when people came to visit the village and so the boat adopted a permanent position right in the middle of the beach.

If you took a right at the junction, the winding road would eventually lead you up the hill to an old wrought iron gate. Beyond the gate lay land which had been left unattended for many years and the remains of what was once the most amazing house for miles around. The owner had been an American business man who had come to Ireland to seek his fortune as a textile merchant.

Once a group of village folk had decided to venture up to the rich American's derelict home out of curiosity. As they approached, they stopped in their tracks for each one felt an eerie force surround them. Terrified, they hurried back to the village, reporting what had just happened. From that day forth, no-one dared to go near the house.

One of the great secrets of Bunbeg was that beyond the site of where the wealthy American used to reside, there lay a path which led to the base of one of the most beautiful mountains ever seen. Errigal. If you looked straight up towards the summit of Errigal, it appeared as if someone had poured fresh cream over the top of the mountain allowing it to drip down, enticing you to stand in awe of its natural beauty.

Mel was usually prepared for the unexpected. Not today. Setting off on her jaunt up to Gallagher's, she resigned herself to masking her true feelings by assuming a fake, uppity manner.

"Here we go again," she muttered, flicking her hair back and developing a slight swagger as she walked. However, on turning the corner at the top of the street, something different met her eyes. Today the crowd was larger than normal and she could see a new gang had arrived. Mel had no idea who they were or where they were from and she really wasn't sure whether to turn around or keep walking. After a few moments, she decided that this little distraction might actually work in her favour. After all, it might mean that the other kids would be otherwise occupied and she could for once buy her sweets without any bother.

As she got closer, it became apparent there was some kind of dispute going on. The locals were standing their ground, making sure the others knew this was their territory and on no account would it be shared with any other gang. Sheepishly, Mel edged her way around the outside of the group, trying not to be noticed. The local kids had formed a circle around the outsiders and some of the boys were starting to push their weight about, throwing shoulders towards each other and leaning forward as a mark of boy power.

Nearly there, she thought, as she eased her way towards the door of Gallagher's.

Then something happened. Something which Mel would remember for the rest of her life.

Someone from the new gang stepped forward. Mel had never set eyes on anyone who looked so mean and threatening. At first she wasn't sure if this was a boy or a girl. Dressed in filthy tracksuit bottoms, football shirt and a white baseball cap turned in reverse, this newcomer had decided enough was enough. She met the tallest and most aggressive of the local kids face to face, who incidentally was not a girl! Staring straight at him she established that this was her show. She would decide when to attack. Everyone froze. Mel dared not make another move, her heart racing with both fear and excitement.

Just when Mel thought she could bear it no longer, the boygirl stepped forward, tilted her head back and with all her might, threw a head butt which hit the local pack leader right between the eyes. For a moment he seemed alright, but slowly his legs weakened and the next thing everyone looked on horrified, as he collapsed to the ground. Gasps could be heard from both gangs as they stared helplessly. Mel's stomach turned as she watched the blood dripping down the side of the boy's face.

Bravely, someone moved forward to help him get back up on his feet, but just as he tried to stand up, the monster lifted her right leg and kicked him straight in the stomach. Faint groans could be heard and then– nothing. That was the worst bit. No movement, no sound – nothing.

A slow smile spread over the boygirl's face as if to signal mission complete. Then the retreat began as she and her followers turned to walk away. Mel felt sick. She wanted to throw up right there, in front of the shop, right in front of all those kids who found her 'odd.' She kept looking at this person lying in front of her, motionless, head cocked to one side, knees pulled forward, eyes closed. She couldn't stand it any longer!

Mustering all the strength in her body she yelled at the boygirl.

"You beast! You all time flaming freak show! Look what you've done!"

The boygirl looked round to see who had dared play with fire. It wasn't too hard to work out, as Mel was now standing on her own, having been abandoned by the others who had all fled.

Trying to remain brave, Mel stood her ground, waiting for the next move. For a moment, time seemed to stand still. Then– boom! The boygirl started to run towards her. Mel took to her heels and ran down the main street as fast as her legs would carry her. Heart racing, gap closing, she took a right at the junction.

Please don't let her catch me!

Mel had never been more frightened in all her life. She could hear the boygirl shouting abuse from behind. How close was she? Not daring to look round, she charged on up the hill, her legs pumping.

If I can just make it to the top, she thought. Remembering how much taller the boygirl was than herself, she feared it was only a matter of time before she would catch up. Just ahead she could see the old iron gate. Would she dare climb over into that unknown territory? There wasn't much choice. She could now hear the sound of running feet behind her. She could practically feel this alien's breath on the back of her neck. Scrambling over the gate, Mel barely noticed the slash down her right shin as she fell to the other side. By now her enemy had caught up and once again they came face to face with each other, the gate being the only thing separating them. Mel was determined that this was not where it was all going to end, with no-one around to help.

Keep going. I'm not giving up now!

And so she continued, breathless, leaping over piles of bricks and rubble, through the estate that once belonged to the rich American. On and on she kept running until she could run no further. Bending over, she gasped desperately for air. Her heart felt like it was going to burst right out of her body. Straightening up, she slowly turned to look behind, petrified of what might meet her eyes, but thankfully it was all clear, the boygirl was nowhere to be seen.

Although Mel had no idea where she was or how far she had run, strangely she felt safe. A warm sensation suddenly filled her body, the fear had gone. As she gathered herself, trying to decide on her next move, she was instantly drawn to what lay ahead. Mel couldn't believe her eyes. Never before had she seen anything more stunning. There in front, rising out of the ground straight up towards the sky, was a mountain of grandeur. Mighty, yet somehow gentle in its simplicity. Rugged beauty, quiet, modest and unassuming. Mel couldn't understand the effect this masterpiece had on her, but one thing she knew for sure - she had been caught. Not by her attacker, but by something much stronger.

Chapter 2

Fresh water. Mel could hear the sound of gurgling water behind her. Turning round, she could see the water trickling past her down towards the village. She watched for a moment, then with a glance, followed the water upstream.

I wonder where it's coming from she thought. Mel concluded it would be madness to return to the village just yet.

Just let things cool down a little, she decided, hoping that the intruders would soon be long gone.

And so she began a gentle climb, following the path of the river in the opposite direction to the flow of the water. The ground was stony and not the easiest to walk on. Mel was poorly prepared for this expedition. The rocks and pot-holes kept getting in the way causing her to fall and eventually lose patience.

That's it! I'm out of here!

Enough was enough. Mel wanted to turn back. Scanning the area, she spotted a little hut over to the right and thought it would be a suitable place to stop and gather her thoughts. Awkwardly, she scrambled over the rocks towards the hut, but as she approached it, something made her realise it was not empty. Although it looked pretty run down on the outside, she could see that the front door had a large brass handle which looked as if it had been carefully polished and there were flower pots crammed with white and yellow daisies on the front doorstep. Pausing, she carefully viewed the hut.

Suddenly she felt a wave of warm air brush across her face. She stood transfixed and closed her eyes in approval. Opening them again, Mel was struck by the sheer beauty. The whole place was now filled with sunlight transforming everything in sight. The river was glistening as it travelled its course, the sky was smooth, electric blue, and the warm air – so captivating!

Mel didn't want to turn back, not yet. With renewed confidence, she walked straight up to the front door and rapped once, twice, then stopped. Nothing. She raised her hand to knock once more, but quickly withdrew it when she heard a low murmur from behind the door.

As she quietly started to back away, she glanced towards the window. One of the curtains started to move. Next, a hand appeared around the side of the curtain and then... a face with accentuated features which made the person look rather odd. However, the quirkiness was masked by a softness which Mel saw in those eyes. She just stared- it took Mel's breath away. A quick look behind her then–where did it go? The face had disappeared. The curtains in place. Not a sound. Mel moved slowly towards the river, not wanting to see anymore.

A massive hand on her shoulder told her to turn around. She obeyed and found she was looking up at that face. No words were exchanged for a few seconds and then pathetically, Mel whimpered, "Please let me go."

The creature quite simply took a deep sigh and with one shake of the head indicated the answer was 'No.'

The sun continued to shine on the back of Mel's neck as she was led into the darkness of the stranger's home.

Mel couldn't quite grasp it. Here she was sitting in a tiny room in a hut, halfway up a mountain, facing the most enormous person she had ever seen. Although uncertain, oddly she felt safe. A few minutes went by and then, in her usual headstrong manner she decided it was time to break the silence.

"My name is Mel. I didn't mean to disturb you, but actually I was being chased by someone and somehow I ended up here. If you don't mind, I should probably be getting back soon."

Mel lowered her head. Suddenly she didn't feel so brave anymore. After what seemed like an eternity, the stranger spoke in the most gentle voice Mel had ever heard.

"I apologise, dear, for frightening you. My name is Wanama and I'm very pleased to meet you. Look at you, you're delightful!" Smiling, she gazed towards the window, then shook her head. After a few seconds she gave a long sigh and continued, "As I was saying, it's such a pleasure to meet you at last. Now, where are my manners? Can I get you something to eat or drink?"

Mel thought hard for a moment. What on earth was she on about?

"Um… no thanks," stammered Mel. " Can I ask, it's just that I was wondering... what exactly do you mean when you say, 'at last'?"

Wanama's eyes stared straight at Mel and then began to disappear as a large smile spread over her face. It was one of those smiles that indicated this was a bright and knowledgeable person who could not be easily fooled.

"My dear, there's a lot for us to talk about. I think you should know something. It's my belief that you were led to me for a reason. I know you'll find it hard to understand just now, but the sooner you start to trust me, the better it will be for both of us."

Changing her tone, she went on, "I must say you're nothing at all like I expected. To be perfectly honest, and please don't be offended, I thought you would've been much taller and stronger looking. However, you don't seem too easily put off by things and that's good."

What the flaming heck! Was this woman for real? Mel dug her nails into her arm to make sure she wasn't dreaming.

This is ridiculous, she thought. Who on earth does this Wanama think she is, presuming she had been led here for some weird reason? What rubbish! If only she had seen how she'd been chased like a rabbit through the town by 'bucket mouth' and how she'd cleverly managed to lose her predator by clambering over the gate. She was seriously out of order. Mel was leaving now and that was that!

She stood up, cleared her throat and in her most polite voice, addressed Wanama.

"I hope you don't mind me saying this, but I really think you've confused me with someone else. You see I live down in the village and I would never normally be anywhere near here only you see..."

But she wasn't allowed to finish. Wanama was shaking her head with that knowing smile again.

"My dear, I hear what you're saying, but you have to listen to me. This is all for real. You've been chosen to do something which no-one else can do. I guess what I'm saying is, you're a very special person. You could make a difference to so many lives."

Mel was struggling to take it all in. She stood up and walked over to the window. The sun glimmered through the trees. The stream glistened as it gurgled over the rocks. Everything outside had a tranquil beauty about it, which was in stark contrast to how Mel felt. Wanama could see she wasn't getting through.

"I realise," she continued, "that no-one can force you to do something you don't believe in, so I want you to go take a walk and think about everything I've said so far. If you decide to ignore what I've said, then I'll accept that. But promise me one thing. Simply ask yourself a question. Ask yourself how many times in life do you get the opportunity to achieve something unique? Something which would give you a clear understanding of who you really are."

Mel was speechless. So much had happened in a very short space of time. Why did things in Mel's life always have to be so complicated? Why couldn't she be like the other kids in the village who seemed to lead such normal lives? Why hadn't she kept her stupid mouth shut when the boy was kicked? Everyone else had. If she hadn't opened her mouth, none of this would have happened. She hated herself. 'Odd Mel!' That's all she'd ever be no

11

matter what this woman said.

She looked at Wanama and gave her that 'I'm sorry for letting you down look,' then turned on her heels and bombed out the door. As she ran down the mountain, it seemed much steeper than before. The warm sun was beating on her back and although it felt good, she couldn't stop. All she wanted to do now was return home where she felt safe, where no-one would tell her lies saying she was special!

"I'M NOT SPECIAL!" she yelled into the silent mountain air. Her face felt cold and wet even though the sun was beating down on her. As she sniffed and wiped her nose, she realised why – she had been crying the whole way down the mountain.

Chapter 3

Wanama wasn't sure how long she'd been sitting staring into space. Eventually she stood up and walked over to the window. The sun was beginning to set behind the trees. With a sigh, she slumped into her chair, reflecting on what a strange day it had been. Her hopes had been both lifted and destroyed by Mel within the space of an hour. This girl could have changed everything. How on earth was she ever going to stop Jezebel now?

Both Wanama and Jezebel had spent all their lives on Errigal, although, for a long time, neither knew of the other's existence. They had always been very different from each other and nothing indicated this more than the fact they lived on opposite sides of the mountain. Wanama lived on the sunny side, while Jezebel lived on the side where the sun never shone. There it was always cold and dreary, just the way Jezebel liked it.

Wanama had lived with her mother enjoying life on this radiant side of the mountain where every day the warm sun spilled her rays transforming everywhere into a place of immaculate beauty. Life here was simple, uncomplicated, perfect.

However, it wasn't long before Wanama noticed she was very different to the others who lived on Errigal. She soon noticed she possessed special healing powers which couldn't be explained. If an animal was injured, she laid a hand on it and it was healed. If a plant was dying, she was able to breathe life back into it. When questioned, her mother simply said that she had a gift as a protector and must use it wisely.

"The time has come for you to use your gift. It's your duty to take care of Errigal and the people around you… you must act as a shield against evil, Wanama, you're the only one who can do this."

Her mother spoke these words in a firm tone which Wanama had never heard before.

The next day she disappeared. Wanama never set eyes on her mother again.

Early one morning, several days later there had been an unexpected knock at the door. For a moment Wanama thought her mother had returned and all would be well again. Eagerly, she opened the door, but was taken aback by what she saw. There, in front of her, was a strange looking man with huge feet and long extended fingers which touched the ground when his arms hung by his side. He appeared somewhat distressed and very short of breath.

"Yeees?" said Wanama. "Can I help?"

"What? Oh yes. You must. Yes, this is very important. Very very important." He spoke so quickly, Wanama could hardly make him out. He saw she was confused.

"Oh I'm hopeless!" and with that he started to cry.

"Hang on," said Wanama gently, "no-one said you were hopeless. Here, come on inside and I'll…"

"NO, NO, NO! There's no time for that!" he yelled as if Wanama was on the other side of the mountain. The weeman seemed to pull himself together and focus again on the job he was sent to do.

"Look here. I've something which I've been instructed to give you. It's really important that we waste no time. There are others who are trying to get this."

Peering over his shoulder he lowered his voice as he continued, "They might even be watching us now. We've got to hurry!"

He took a small pouch out of his pocket and held it up for Wanama to see. Wanama reached for it, trying to make sense of what he was telling her, but he quickly drew back.

"Listen. Inside this pouch is something very valuable. It possesses a power which can only be released by someone with a special gift."

He paused for a moment, slightly nervous about what he was going to say next. "You have that gift."

Wanama was beginning to think the weeman was completely out of his mind. She had had enough.

"Look, you must go now." She began to close the door, but before she knew it, he had thrust himself forward, wedging his foot between her and the door.

"Shut up and listen, will you!"

This man was going nowhere until he had completed what he had set out to do. Nervously she opened the door a little further. He had her full attention.

"The Blue Stone has remained hidden until now. In one week at precisely midnight, Sirius, the brightest star, will appear directly above Errigal. The Blue Stone must be in the direct path of its light. The light from Sirius will activate The Blue Stone, giving the person who is holding it complete control of the mountain. Only a few people hold this power... You are one of the few. Over time, the power will become stronger and eventually you could have complete control over Errigal and beyond."

The weeman stopped for a moment allowing the enormity of what he'd said to sink in. Placing his hand over his mouth, he shook his head, for he didn't quite know how he was going to fully explain the importance of what he'd been sent to do. Raising his head, he looked Wanama directly in the eyes and swallowed hard.

"What I'm saying Wanama, is that it's very important you don't mess up! Understood?"

Wanama was a little dazed to say the least, but nevertheless took the pouch from the weeman and felt inside. She touched something very smooth and round, no bigger than a marble. Lifting it out, she studied it carefully expecting to find something quite extraordinary, but all she saw was a blue stone. That was it? And this was supposed to hold a powerful force?

"I don't really understand," said Wanama looking at him suspiciously. "Why do you think I should be the possessor of The Stone?"

"Because"... (By now he was completely frustrated as this had all taken much longer than he'd anticipated!) He took a deep breath and in a much calmer voice explained,

"Because you are one of the few who have the gift to release the power. You can do things which others can't do, like heal animals and bring plants back to life. Your mother recognised your gift when you were very young."

Wanama turned away. The mention of her mother

filled her with a deep sadness. Shaking her head she looked down at the weeman and quietly inquired,

"Did my mum know about The Stone?"

He nodded sadly. "Your Mum knew they were coming for The Stone."

"Who?"

"THEM! Those beasts on the other side. She didn't want to put your life at risk so she gave it to me to keep it safe as part of her plan."

"What plan?"

He swallowed hard before continuing. "She couldn't take a chance on you being taken prisoner so, your Mum gave herself up. She told them that she would lead them to The Blue Stone. It was so brave of her."

His voice drifted off as he hung his head, reflecting on her tremendous courage "But of course she had no intention of handing over The Stone. She'd already given it to me along with instructions to deliver it to you after she'd gone."

By now Wanama was fighting back the tears. The weeman found it difficult to watch this giant of a woman crumble before his eyes.

"Can you please tell me what happened to my Mum?"

Although Wanama wasn't sure she wanted to hear the truth, she knew she had to know it to help her understand what all this meant. She knelt before him, their eyes level, imploring him to explain.

"Please," she begged.

Reluctantly he continued.

"She told the Jebelites, the ones who'd come over from

the other side of the mountain, that she'd hidden The Stone in an opening at the top of Errigal. They forced her to show them where it was and said that if it wasn't there they'd come back for you. She would never let that happen. I made sure I was nearby to help with the plan. Anyway, when they reached the top, she took them over to a rock. This rock covered an opening which dropped right into the heart of Errigal... thousands of feet below. Your Mum's plan was to pretend to slip as she climbed down the opening to get The Stone. The idea was that one of the Jebelites would lean over to help her, because of- course they needed your Mum to show them where The Stone was hidden. Your Mum would then pull the Jebelite down with her and I would step in and push the other to his death."

"Oh dear God!" gasped Wanama. "Is that what happened?"

"Well, not exactly. When I ran over for my part, the Jebelite must have become suspicious, because he swung round just as I was about to push him over the edge. Startled, he took off and before I knew it he was well out of sight."

Wanama could hardly take in what he was now saying. The shock of finding out what her mother had done and how bravely she'd sacrificed herself, hit right to the core of her soul. Burying her head in her hands, she moaned like a little child.

"Why her?"

"Look, I know it's hard for you to understand, but you must listen carefully."

He took Wanama's hand in his long fingers and gently

lifted them from her weeping eyes.

"Can we sit down for a moment?" Although time was running out, the weeman could see that Wanama was struggling with what she had just heard. He felt sorry for this woman who at first had appeared huge and strong, but was now so fragile. He led her to a chair and they both sat down at the table where Wanama's cup of tea sat cooling. With some urgency he continued.

"This Jebelite is on the run. It's only a matter of time before he comes here looking for The Stone. He's already stepped over to this side which means he can't return to the dark side of Errigal. You can be sure Jezebel will use him to get what she wants. You must keep The Stone well hidden and make sure you trust no-one. In seven days, Sirius will pass above Errigal and shine down unlocking its power. Keep vigilant till then."

Anticipating a shower of questions, the weeman took a step back and just as quickly as he appeared, he vanished, leaving Wanama stunned by what she'd just been told.

Within moments she was sobbing tears of grief for her mother. She knew now she was gone for good. She sprawled her arms across the table as she wept, confused about what to do next. How would she manage to do this on her own?

Her thoughts were quickly interrupted by a faint sound from behind. She swung round just in time to see The Blue Stone roll off the table, onto the floor and under a chair. Hurrying quickly over to the chair, she knelt down and rummaged around, her fingers searching desperately for The Stone. She stretched her arm out as far as she could, terrified she'd lost it. After a few moments of grasping madly in thin air, she felt something cold and smooth and quickly closed her hand tightly around it before it had a chance to roll away again. But something was beside The Stone – there was a piece of paper right next to it. She pulled the two things out together and soon realised this was no accident.

Written on the paper was a clear message to Wanama.

My Dearest Wanama,

It's in your possession. Don't let it go. The power of The Blue Stone now belongs to you. Even though you may feel alone, remember, I'm with you in spirit..... I'll never leave you. I'm sorry my darling I had to depart so suddenly, but I hope, with time, you'll understand. Until then, put your trust in The Blue Stone of Errigal.

Mum xxx

Chapter 4

Wanama's head began to spin. Staggering across the room, she collapsed into her chair, clutching The Stone with all her might, dazed and weak from the sudden realisation that, held tightly in her grasp, was a tiny object of the most enormous magnitude.

She had never felt more alone in all her life and wanted desperately to understand what this all meant. However, one thing she was sure about – The Stone must be kept safe. Errigal was a mountain full of mystery and wonder and one of these mysteries was the strange folk who lived in the unexplored depths of the mountain. Wanama didn't want to take any risks. She would hide it away for now, until she needed it in seven days' time when Sirius was due to appear, so she had carefully put The Stone into a wooden box and placed it in the back of the drawer of her sewing table.

The next day she decided to wander down to take a drink from the fresh mountain water. Kneeling, she cupped her hands and dipped them into the cool water, but looking down she noticed unusual shapes, squirming to and fro as if trying desperately to reach the surface. She leant over to get a closer look, her face practically touching the water now. There was definitely something going on below, but it all looked a little blurry. Suddenly, there was an explosion of water and the next thing Wanama knew, she was completely showered in icy cold water! Dripping wet, she blinked several times to try to bring herself back to reality. What on earth had just happened? The river was always calm. It never changed, constant, just like the mountain. Her attention was drawn to a large rock at the edge of the river, where the strangest looking fish were slithering around. They were all the same colour, a shade of deep purple, each one with an enormous tail about three times the size of its body, almost blinding to look at as they shimmered and glistened in the morning sun. One by one the fish moved towards Wanama and the next thing she knew, she was surrounded by about fifty of the odd little creatures. One, which seemed to glisten more than the rest, wriggled up Wanama's leg and onto her knee. She stayed very still, afraid to move in case she might harm the water creature. Slowly, the fish raised its body upwards and, balancing firmly on its tail, faced Wanama eye to eye! With one long sharp intake of breath, it spoke,

"Something awful has happened. Oh Wanama, Jezebel has managed to drive all the mountain folk to her side. You're the only one who has been spared!"

"What are you talking about?" cried Wanama, trying to catch her breath.

"One of the Jebelites has been hiding here. He tricked the children into stepping across the summit. When their parents and families realised what had happened they couldn't bear to be apart from them."

"You're saying they followed them over – into Jezebel's world of darkness?" Wanama couldn't believe what she was hearing.

" They had no choice – they had to go."

Before anyone had a chance to say anymore, they were interrupted by a high pitched shriek which could be heard from the trees on the other side of the river. It was the weeman.

"Wanama, oh my heavens, Wanama!" hc gasped.

Plunging into the river, he swam as quickly as his long arms would let him. Clambering out on her side, he gave himself a shake then ran full pelt towards her. He came to an abrupt halt right in front of her nearly causing an unpleasant collision. Did this creature ever slow down?

"I TOLD YOU TO TAKE CARE OF THAT STONE! DIDN'T YOU HEAR ME? IT COULDN'T HAVE BEEN MORE SIMPLE. YOU'VE LET ME DOWN...AND NOW THAT BEAST HAS IT! HOW COULD YOU HAVE LET THIS HAPPEN! How could you?"

As his voice trailed off, he sunk his tiny face into his hands and sobbed. Wanama had never heard crying like it.

"What do you mean? Who has The Stone?" she gasped.

Taking both hands in hers, she looked him straight in the eyes and repeated in a calmer voice, "Now tell me, who has The Stone?"

The weeman stopped crying and suddenly his expression changed. He screwed up his face and with venom and hatred in his voice, whispered a name which was seldom mentioned on this side of the mountain, "Jezebel!"

A fearful silence fell. Wanama walked back and forward, shaking her head trying to think of a way out of this mess. A few minutes passed then one of the fish piped up,

"Wait a minute!" He swiftly wriggled his way to the

front. "There is a way. Listen, we all know that to cross Errigal's summit means no return for us... but what about the villagers? They can step over onto either side. If we can get one of them to work for us, someone we could trust, well, they could get The Stone back. That would surely work. What do you think?"

Feeling very pleased with himself, he slithered back to the other fish.

One of the larger fish finally spoke. Perching himself on a rock directly in front of Wanama he raised his gleaming purple fin in the air and smiled.

"You know, I think that might work. We could use the spirits of the mountain to help lead someone from the village to you, Wanama. Someone who is strong, who can be trusted."

And so that was how it came about that Mel was led to Wanama in the hope that she could help save Errigal by going in search of The Blue Stone.

Chapter 5

Back in the village Mel felt sick. Not in the sense that she wanted to throw up, but more like how you feel when you are missing home. No matter what she did, she couldn't shake this feeling off. She tried rearranging her room, counting up and sorting all the loose coins she could find under her bed, filling her calendar with all the dates of special events (not that there were too many for her to worry about) and as a last resort, offered to help her mum put away the shopping.

"What's up with you today?" inquired her mum, as she shoved the weekly supply of ham, bacon and cheese into the already jam-packed fridge.

"Nothing," sighed Mel, who was well practised in with–holding her true feelings. Balancing a pile of groceries in her arms and barely able to see above the packets of food, Mel couldn't help wondering why Mums always seem to feel a measure of their brilliance is based on the amount of food they buy. She tried her best to steady the pile of shopping in her arms. However, attempting to open the door of the fridge proved too difficult and the whole lot fell to the floor. Staring at the mess of splattered yoghurts and eggs in front of her, she glanced at her mum who was clearly not amused!

"For heaven's sake, Mel! Will you ever learn? Can't you even do a simple thing like put the shopping away without causing chaos? Honestly, sometimes I wonder where on earth you came from... on you go!" Waving her arms she continued,

"Get out of here! Go on! I'm better off doing these things on my own."

Reality check.

Mel couldn't help feeling that she was continually misunderstood by everyone. Even her own Mum didn't seem to truly understand her. Why was it that people seemed to jump to conclusions about her, assuming she didn't have feelings just because she didn't fulfil the criteria of 'a typical 12 year old.' Why did people insist on dictating to her like she was some sort of brainless device that could be programmed to do whatever someone else decided. Well, she'd had enough!

The events which happened over the next few minutes changed Mel's life forever.

She turned to her Mum and in a deep, controlled voice said, "You know what? You're right Mum. You're better off doing things on your own. I'm out of here!"

And with that, Mel shot out the front door leaving her mother speechless at her daughter's sudden outburst. After a few moments, her Mum reassured herself that it would only be a matter of time before she would come running back with some tearful apology. As she carried on cleaning up the mess Mel had left behind, she went on muttering to herself. "Really! That girl needs reined in. Wait till I see her later. We're going to have to do some serious talking about her behaviour. The joys of bringing that child up on my own!"

By now Mel was running at top speed down the street. She didn't even glance in the direction of Gallagher's as she flew past. Slowing down to catch her breath, she threw a backward glance towards the old fishing boat on the beach, then quickly sped off, slicing the corner as she scooted up the hill towards the iron gates. Without a second thought, Mel dived over the gate and ran on until she could run no more. And there it was again.

The silence, warmth, calmness.

Suddenly everything seemed different. Here she was once more, at the base of Errigal.

She felt protected, at home. The sickness had gone!

Mel found herself standing in front of Wanama's little hut. She stared for a short time, not quite sure of how she was going to explain her reason for returning. She needn't have worried because, within seconds, Wanama was standing in front of her, smiling that warm, knowing smile which Mel found so comforting.

"I'd hoped you would come back," Wanama said softly.

Mel paused for a moment then in her usual brash manner, explained to Wanama that she didn't want to hang about and could she please just tell her what it was she had to do that was so important.

Slowly Wanama led Mel inside and sat her down while she explained everything. Mel listened carefully as she was told about The Blue Stone of Errigal and how it had come to be stolen.

"Jezebel, who lives on the other side of the mountain, now has The Stone. The power inside it can only be released from the light of Sirius, the brightest star in the Galaxy. It's only a matter of days before Sirius will appear directly above the summit of Errigal and the power can be released. Only problem is, the person holding The Blue Stone at the crucial moment when Sirius sheds its light, is the one who will have complete control of Errigal. So, I'm sure you understand how important it is for The Stone to end up in the right hands."

Mel, completely intrigued by what she was being told, didn't mutter a single word. She was waiting to find out what her part would be in all of this.

Wanama went on to explain how she needed someone to climb to the top of Errigal then cross over to Jezebel's side of the mountain.

"You see, the problem for us is that if anyone from my side of the mountain crosses the summit of Errigal, there's no return. Once they've entered the darkness of Errigal, they remain under Jezebel's rule."

"Ok. So what exactly are you saying here?" Mel looked suspisciously at Wanama.

This wasn't going to be easy. Wanama didn't quite know how to put it without frightening Mel.

"I need you to go over to get The Stone."

"What? You must be joking. No way – I can't do it!"

"Yes you can. You're a villager. You can go over to Jezebel's side AND return back to us. You see Mel, you are our only hope of getting The Stone back."

Mel's eyes dropped to the floor. She was speechless. The thought of going into the unknown, where there was nothing but darkness, to retrieve a Stone which held a strong force... this was asking the impossible.

In an attempt to put her at ease, Wanama reassured her that she would be safe as far as the top of Errigal.

"Some of the creatures who live around here will stay with you until you cross over to the other side."

She paused.

"Mel, you don't know what this would mean to us."

She hung her head waiting for her reply.

Mel didn't know what to think. Part of her felt moved that someone actually thought her important enough to complete such a task and yet deep down she was terrified.

"I need some time to think this through," she said quietly.

"I understand." Wanama could already detect a great strength in this girl and was growing fonder of her by the minute. She watched her step out the door into the sunlight and walk down the path.

Mel stood at the bottom of the path and stared up at the blinding sun. Gazing at the stream of sunlight, she closed her eyes and felt the heat penetrate her body. Then something odd happened. Try as she might, Mel couldn't move a single muscle. She was acutely aware of a strange sensation travelling through her. It felt as if her whole body had become engulfed in some kind of mysterious force. She stiffened for a few moments then, the force shot out leaving her feeling weak and confused. She stumbled forward, slightly disorientated, rubbing her eyes in an attempt to make sense of what she had experienced. Turning round, she found Wanama standing at the door of her house, watching. Her head was spinning making her feel like she was going to pass out. She closed her eyes again and suddenly everything became clear.

Walking up the path at a quick pace, Mel took a deep

breath. She approached the doorway and stopped right in front of Wanama.

"Okay, I'll do it. I'll get it back for you."

They stood facing each other for a few brief seconds then Wanama broke the silence.

"Thank you Mel. Thank you so much."

Afraid she might change her mind, Mel quickly stepped into action.

"Ok. Tell me when you want me to go."

"We have to act quickly, before it's too late. There's no time to lose. Wait here and I'll call the helpers together to get you safely to the top of the mountain."

Taking hold of her hands she spoke in a soft voice as she continued,

"Listen to me. Once you cross over, don't be afraid. Even though you can't see me, I'll be there in spirit, guiding you. Just try to keep to the path. It will eventually lead you to Jezebel's cave. The Stone will be hidden there. She'll not want to be too far from it, so you'll have to watch her carefully to find out where exactly she's hidden it. I know it's a lot to ask but try not to be frightened. There are folk over there who will want to help you, people who used to live on my side of the mountain."

Wanama made a high pitched whistle which startled Mel.

"It's my signal to the meerkats," she explained.

"Don't worry. They're smart creatures. I promise they'll get you safely to the top."

Feeling light–headed she tried to make sense of what Wanama was saying. Meerkats? What on earth were they? Across the stream at the edge of the forest, she could just about make out a sandy coloured feline shape, stretched in an upright position, perched on its hind legs. It pointed its nose in the air and made a couple of sharp barking sounds. Within seconds a gang of similar creatures appeared from little openings in the ground. They quickly gathered around their leader. Then, with another loud bark, they sprung into action. Mel had never seen anything like it. She glanced at Wanama who was standing silently, watching them dart over rocks and bushes with such ease.

As they slowed to a halt at the water's edge, Wanama gave another whistle and Mel watched in amazement as one by one they leapt across the stream. They were the most athletic creatures she had ever seen!

Before she knew it, the whole gang was standing in front of her, their beady black eyes staring straight up at Wanama waiting to be told why they had been summoned.

Mel listened as Wanama gave them clear instructions about how to ensure Mel's safety, reminding them of how much she was depending on them. She could feel her body shake as she listened to Wanama explain the importance of her job.

"Now go. There's no time to waste."

Turning to Mel she smiled.

"Here, take this." She placed the shawl she had been wearing over her shoulders. "Remember, I'll be with you every step of the way."

Mel had so many questions to ask but she knew there was no time. No goodbyes, no hugs. Wanama just stood there as Mel turned, gave a quick wave and set off surrounded by the meerkats. Although she knew she had been given a strength from somewhere, Mel couldn't help but wonder how she was going to manage this.

The truth was, Wanama couldn't bring herself to say goodbye. She truly didn't know if she would ever see Mel again.

The journey to the top of the mountain wasn't quite as exhausting as Mel thought it might be. The meerkats dutifully led her to the highest point of Errigal.

"Okay, this is as far as we go," announced Theo who seemed to be the leader. "You're on your own from here."

The abrupt halt from the mountain animals indicated that their part in assisting her had come to an end. They gazed at Mel as if to kindly reassure her and kneeling down, she reached out in a gesture of thanks to each of them, then turned round to face the side of Errigal which was feared by so many. Taking a deep breath before beginning her descent, she looked back to wave goodbye to her companions. But her heart sank when she glanced round to see that every one of them had disappeared – back to where they belonged, fearful of getting too close to the darkness which lay just over the top of the mountain. She was alone. She glanced back. Everything as far as the eye could see, sparkled in the sunlight. The trees in the forest became vibrant as the light streamed through each one of them.

Hesitating for a moment, she quietly reminded herself of the importance of what had to be done. One thing was certain - she definitely wasn't going back now.

And so with one deep breath, Mel took her first step across the summit into the dark unknown.

Chapter 6

It was like entering a different world. One step over the summit and Mel was engulfed by darkness. Rubbing her arms for heat and comfort, she felt an odd sharpness in the air. To her left, she could just about make out clusters of trees which seemed to reach right up into the night sky. Best avoid the forest, she reckoned. I need to find the path.

Ahead there were bushes everywhere, no evidence of a path in sight. The only way Mel reckoned she was going to make any headway was by battling her way through them. This was clearly not going to be easy, especially for someone like Mel who always tried to steer clear of outdoor pursuits!

After fighting her way through numerous thistle bushes, it wasn't long before Mel felt like packing it all in. Unable to keep her balance, she slid smack into a large rock! There must be an easier way to get down this blasted mountain, she thought.

Slowly gathering herself together, she stood up and looked ahead. There wasn't a lot to see. Masses of rocky wasteland covered with a splattering of prickly bushes. It was impossible to see more than a few feet ahead because of the enormous dark shadow over the mountain.

Without any warning, she felt a wave of fear ripple right through her body. The reality of what she was doing had finally hit her. No–one to turn to for help or advice – just the knowledge that she had been chosen to complete this task for reasons better known to others than to herself.

In spite of how she was feeling, she continued, but it wasn't long before the wind picked up. The sky darkened and soon the rain was beating down so hard that Mel had to shield her face, unable to see a thing. She knelt down by a large bush, trying to shelter from the rainstorm. She reached for the scarf Wanama had given her and pulled it out of her pocket to wrap around her head and shoulders. It smelt of the other side of the mountain.

Should she wait for the darkness to lift? Should she turn back or yell for help at the top of her voice?

There was something moving above her. At first it was difficult to make out if it was just the heavy rain. She turned around, but couldn't see a thing. There it was again. This time it narrowly skimmed past her ear. She wrapped her arms around her head, burying her face in her chest, hoping that whatever it was would go away. But it didn't. As she unravelled her arms, she felt a quick blast of air and something hairy touch her cheek as it whisked past. She jumped up. The creature was flying. She had to escape before it attacked her.

Peering into the darkness, she started to walk. Her pace quickened as she felt sure this 'thing' was following her.

Her heart was racing as she tried to think of how to escape from the beast, but suddenly the direction of the wind changed and Mel could hear a gentle voice instructing her.

"Straight ahead... keep going... next large rock..."

Mel followed the whispered instructions, trying not to fall or bump into anything. She made her way to the rock, then stopped. She sat down on top of it for a moment to catch her breath and instantly noticed how unsteady it was. Slithering off, she gave it a gentle push, astonished to find how easy it was to shift. The next thing she knew the rock was moving by itself, revealing a large open space beneath. Mel looked down and had to rub her eyes as the light streamed straight up towards her. Her instinct told her this was a safe place.

There were little steps leading downwards which Mel quickly used, hoping all the time that the flying creature which had tormented her earlier, was well out of range. As she made it to the bottom, she was startled by a loud sound from above. The rock was sliding across the opening, cutting out all the darkness, trapping her under the ground! At that moment the whole place filled with chatter. Mel spun round and could hardly believe her eyes. The place was overcrowded with ants. Everywhere. They were moving around so rapidly, none of them seemed to even notice she was there.

Mel cleared her throat in an attempt to get their attention. In unison they stopped what they were doing as if they had been cleverly choreographed, weaving in the same direction, at the same speed towards Mel, whose eyes were growing wider by the second!

However, she needn't have feared. The Queen Ant commanded silence and all obeyed.

"Don't be afraid, Mel. We know about you and believe me, you need our help. There are many forces working against you, but equally many working for you. Listen. This is a safe place for now. None of the Jebelites can get you here. But unfortunately you can't stay for long.

It's vital that you get to The Blue Stone before Jezebel realises what's happening. It's only a matter of time before she finds out. We'll look after all your needs so that you can continue safely on your way."

Swallowing hard, Mel politely addressed her audience.

"Well, thank you. I really don't know what else to say. You're very kind taking me into your um...home."

Smiling, the Queen moved a little closer to Mel. The other ants, in an act of approval, formed a large ring around their visitor as if to reassure her that they wanted to protect her and be her friend.

As she looked at her new surroundings she let out a deep sigh.

"This is all a bit strange for me, but I really appreciate what you've done. I dread to think what would have happened if I hadn't found this hideaway. Anyway I'll try not to disrupt your busy routine too much!"

Mel had their full attention and for the first time in her life she felt important. With an awkward, half smile she continued, "If you don't mind, I'd give anything for something to eat right now– if that's not too much trouble."

Straight away the army of ants did an about turn and without being told, Mel knew to follow. They led her to a room with a wooden table covered in vegetable leaves and berries. Mel forced a smile, attempting to hide her true feelings about the feast in front of her.

"Help yourself to whatever you want," came a little voice from one of the ants which had broken away from the crowd and was now crawling up Mel's leg. Normally

this wouldn't have been a pleasant experience for her, but she couldn't help feeling a strange attachment to her new friends.

The ants scurried around frantically preparing food. It looked totally unappetising but Mel had become so hungry and her hosts had obviously gone to great trouble that she decided to sample some. She bravely lifted what looked like a cabbage leaf and took a nibble. It was delicious! The first bite tasted of roast beef, the second of roast potatoes. She tucked in and polished off the whole plate within minutes, then moved on to the berries which tasted of strawberries and cream and chocolate sauce, all in one. She licked her lips, her hunger satisfied for now. The ants kept guard until she had finished, then in true military style, they reorganised themselves into a straight line and led Mel to another chamber. As she peered in, her eyes grew wide. There in front of her was a room which had been carefully prepared, just for her. And beside what looked like a bed of moss draped with a soft blue quilt, was a photograph of someone who Mel recognised right away – Wanama. Lifting it up, she gazed at it for a few moments then set it down again.

"You know, I'm shattered! Would you mind if I turned in for the night?"

Within seconds the ants had disappeared and left Mel alone. As she pulled the quilt over her, she looked again at the photo of the person who had asked so much of her. Staring at the photo, she wondered how she had ever got herself into this.

Her head nestled into the clean dry moss and as she

started to drift off Mel was sure she could hear the gentle sound of Wanama's voice comforting her as she settled into a deep sleep.

Chapter 7

"Crazy! Crazy!" screeched Jezebel at the top of her voice. "HOW MANY?"

"Only one, a young girl," came a timid reply from the crowd of Jebelites who had been instructed to gather for an emergency meeting in Jezebel's gloomy, damp cave.

"How could this have happened? How has she managed to make it so far down the mountain without getting caught?"

Screwing up her face she leant towards her people.

"Someone had better come up with answers... NOW!"

Scanning the crowd, her eye was drawn to a young man who was huddled close to his wife and son.

"Well? YOU!" she shouted, pointing at him. "Tell me, what's your name, my dear?" Jezebel suddenly switched to a sweeter, yet still unsettling tone of voice.

"Zurin, M'am," came back the reply.

"Well, Zurin since you, among others, don't appear to have done much to prevent this girl from making her way across MY territory, you now have the honour of being put in charge of bringing her to me. Do you understand what I'm demanding of you?"

Noticing how uneasy Zurin looked, she sneered, mocking him.

"Let's see. Just to make sure there's no mis-understanding between us – I instruct you to capture the girl and bring her to me... Oh how I'll enjoy punishing the devious little brat once I've got everything out of her!"

Rubbing her hands together in anticipation of what

was to come she carried on, "Are we clear now, Zurin?"

"Um, yes– If you're sure that's what you want, M'am."

Taking a step forward, Jezebel rolled her eyes in disbelief.

"Excuse me. 'If I'm sure that's what I want?' " she mimicked, astounded at what she'd just heard. "You have a nerve, young man, to doubt anything I ask of you. Let's just remind ourselves who's in charge around here."

With a click of her fingers, a multitude of bats swept into the cave, flying upwards as each found a place to perch. Most of the Jebelites by now were so scared they could hardly move. No-one dared look up at the black creatures hanging above them.

Jezebel was finding it hard to contain her anger. Zurin had far too much compassion to make him a worthy Jebelite. She needed someone she could rely on, especially now that The Blue Stone was under threat. Someone who was prepared to do whatever she commanded, regardless of the consequences. Rubbing her chin, she narrowed her eyes as she thought of her next move.

"Come closer, young man," she spoke softly as she summoned him up onto the platform where she was standing.

Zurin looked at his wife who was now sobbing, clinging to their son who had his arms wrapped tightly around her waist. He took his wife's hand and gave it a gentle squeeze.

"I'll be alright," he reassured her, forcing a smile.

Stepping up onto the platform, he found himself face to face with the person he feared most.

"Now, what's your name again?"

"Zurin, M'am."

"Ah yes, Zurin. You're a bit of a disappointment to me.

44

A real disappointment."

Shaking her head, she hesitated for a brief moment, staring at Zurin who was now petrified at what was coming next.

"You see, Zurin I don't wait around for losers. In fact, come to think of it, I really don't need pathetic weaklings like you on MY MOUNTAIN! DO YOU HEAR ME YOU? DO YOU?"

By now Jezebel could not contain her temper. It poured out of her toes as she stamped her feet and through her fingers as she flung her fists into the air, screaming at the top of her voice.

Zurin had never been more frightened in all his life. Biting the inside of his cheek, he tried his best to remain calm. Sensing time was running out, he courageously stepped towards her,

"I didn't mean to upset you, M'am. Just tell me what you want me to do. Please, give me a chance. I have a wife and child."

Calming down for a moment, there was a hint of some compassion from Jezebel.

"Oh, I see a wife and child. How nice for you, Zurin. They're going to just love what I have planned for you."

"Nooooo!" A desperate shout could be heard from the crowd. It was Zurin's wife. "Leave him alone, please, I'm begging you!"

Ignoring her pleas, Jezebel threw her head back and let out a shriek of laughter, which even startled the bats who were sleepily settling on the rafters above. Then, without warning her voice changed.

"Say good-bye to your dear wife and child, you pitiful being! Let's hope they show me more strength than you did!"

Showing no mercy, she clicked her fingers once again, giving a command which sent ripples of shock throughout the crowd.

"He's all yours!"

Straight away a flurry of bats descended, surrounding him quicker than you could imagine. No-one really knew what was happening, but when the bats departed all they could see that was left of Zurin were the clothes he had been wearing. He was gone.

Zurin's wife fell to her knees, numb from what she had just witnessed. Matthieu, her son, couldn't contain himself.

"You monster! What have you done to my dad?"

Running through the crowd, he grabbed his Dad's clothes and held them up for her to see. "What have you done to him?"

His voice trailed off as he buried his face in all that remained of the person he most admired in the entire world. His muffled cries could be heard throughout the cave, yet no-one had the courage to go over to him.

Rising to his feet, Matthieu threw a threatening glance at Jezebel, "You'll pay for this!" And with that he took to his heels and charged out of the cave. The bats gathered, waiting for their next instruction, but their leader just shook her head.

"Leave him. He's not worth it. He's just a child. I'll deal with him later."

Everyone stood in shocked silence until Jezebel decided to speak again.

"So, we are now clear. I make the rules and you obey. Right?"

"Yes, M'am," came a chorus of voices from the crowd.

"Have I any volunteers to take the job on or do I have to call you up one by one to suffer the same fateful end as Zurin?"

You could feel the unease in the air. Most of the Jebelites looked down as if hopeful they would find some kind of strength from beneath. An icy chill swept throughout the cave as everyone became acutely aware of Jezebel's growing impatience.

Just as people were starting to accept the inevitable, a voice could be heard from the middle of the crowd.

"I'll do it."

Jezebel stretched forward to try to see who had addressed her with such confidence.

"Get up here whoever you are. Let me take a look at you."

Slowly, a tall thin girl stepped out from the crowd. Not too pretty. In fact there was nothing very feminine about her at all. She walked right up to Jezebel, staring her straight in the eyes,

"I'll do it."

"Ah yes, Sam, such a gallant gesture."

Jezebel knew this girl. She had come to Errigal from the village.One of the few villagers who'd ever made it onto the mountain. She, of course, looked very different from the other Jebelites, but that didn't matter. Jezebel wanted this girl for one obvious reason- she could cross over to the other side of Errigal. This could be very useful for Jezebel, especially now that The Blue Stone was under threat.

"What makes you think you're up to this?" Jezebel needed to be sure she was equal to the task.

"Because, I have a motive to do it."

"Oh and what would that be?" asked Jezebel who was becoming more and more curious.

"I want you to give me a position of authority under your rule, M'am. I won't disappoint you. I really want to prove my worth. Please give me a chance."

Jezebel stared at the girl. Some thought she was going to explode. No-one had ever dared to demand anything from Jezebel before. But, surprisingly Jezebel remained calm. She thought hard about this request. Did she really believe someone else could help her govern her mountain? She had to admit this girl had guts. This was exactly the kind of person Jezebel was looking for. Perhaps she could help her increase her power, especially if she could cross over to the other side. If she gave her a position of authority, well two would be stronger and better than one. A smile stole across Jezebel's face. "Very well. Let's see what you're made of. If you get rid of our imposter, you work with me rather than for me."

Somewhat taken aback by the speed at which Jezebel accepted her offer, the girl continued.

"Thank you. I'll not disappoint you, M'am."

As she began to take her place back among the people, Jezebel shouted, "Wait!"

The girl spun round and looked her directly in the face.

"A warning, my dear. If you let me down, your punishment

will be so great that you'll be begging me to give you the same treatment I gave to Zurin!"

Chapter 8

"This is an impossible situation. It would be like handing her a death sentence. The place is crawling with Jezebel's messengers."

The ants couldn't decide on a plan of action. They agreed about most things, but right now there was a split in the ranks. Should they ask Mel to leave before it was too late?

The Queen Ant had called a special meeting in the early hours of the morning to come up with a plan.

A few of the braver ones dared to speak out.

"She's not prepared for tackling the journey on her own."

"That's right," agreed one of the others.

"It was alright when Jezebel didn't know she'd made it across the summit, but not now."

A multitude of tiny black heads nodded in unison.

It was true. Jezebel wouldn't take any chances. She knew Mel was working her way towards The Blue Stone and she'd do whatever she had to in order to keep The Stone safe.

However, the ants also knew that if it was discovered they were working against Jezebel it would be curtains for them! As it was, Jezebel knew nothing about them. They were safe underground, well away from her cruel dictatorship.

"She can't stay here. It's as simple as that! She's got to leave before she puts all of us at risk, as well as herself."

No-one wanted to make things any more difficult for Mel than they already were, but everyone agreed their lives were now in danger.

"Listen," piped up one of the ants, "we could still help her."

All heads turned towards one of the littlest ants, positioned right at the back of the gathering.

"We know the underground route to Jezebel's cave, right?"

They all nodded in agreement.

"Well, if we churn up the soil under the ground's surface, we could map out the route for Mel, a route which Jezebel wouldn't expect her to follow. She'll be expecting Mel to follow the path."

The Queen Ant appeared to be mulling this idea over. Her eyelids closed slowly over her protruding eyes as she held her arm up for quiet. It was hard to tell if she'd risk continuing to play a part in helping Mel. Jezebel didn't know anything about their existence and that was how she wanted it to remain.

"Right. We're done talking," she said, coming back to reality. "Time to vote. Raise your head, all those in favour of helping Mel on her journey to Jezebel's cave."

Mel woke early the next morning. Even if she'd wanted to, she couldn't have slept much longer. There was the sound of hard work all around her. The ants were racing round tidying, preparing food and generally organising themselves. Mel rose from her bed and walked timidly over to the door. She peered out into the long empty corridor. Silence. Where were all those busy bodies she heard a few minutes ago? Before she had time to turn around, the corridor was covered in a carpet of ants. It was as if someone had just poured them like water out of a jug. Mel was afraid that if she stood for too long she would be completely submerged in them! She quickly closed the door, raced back into bed and clambered under the sheets in an attempt to escape the multitude of little maniacs who were advancing towards her room.

For a while everything seemed to be quite normal again. Mel plucked up the courage to emerge from under the sheets and sat up breathing a sigh of relief. As she started to relax and think about her plans, she could see a dark shadow growing across the bottom of the door.

"What's all this?" she muttered. In a matter of seconds the ants were racing under the door and soon covered the floor of Mel's room. She couldn't believe how quickly they shifted. And, amazingly, they could stop with the same speed. Right at the tips of her toes, the ants froze. The others who were behind, immediately followed the command and all came to an abrupt standstill.

"Well," gasped Mel. "That was some performance!"

There was a lot of chattering among the tiny black creatures and then one of them crawled up Mel's leg and began to speak.

"It's time for you to go. We've done all we can for you now. Take the food we've packed and carry on with your journey. We would love to have you for longer, but time is running out. Jezebel knows you're on her part of the mountain."

The ants all stared at Mel and could see she was afraid.

"Look, we know this isn't easy for you, but you've got to keep going. We're going to help you Mel. Just follow the mounds of dirt we make along the ground. This route should buy you some time before Jezebel's messengers find you again. We'll take you within reach of Jezebel's cave. After that you're on your own." Sensing her anguish, one of the ants drew close to her.

"It'll be ok Mel, just remain alert at all times. Don't forget, not everyone is working for her ladyship!"

She felt a great sense of warmth. These folk had not stopped doing things for her since she had arrived the night before. In all the years she had lived down in the village, no-one had ever displayed such kindness towards her.

"You're right. I must get on my way. You've all been so good to me. I really appreciate the risk you're taking in helping me on my way. I'll honestly never forget this."

As she rose to collect her things, they respectfully cleared a pathway for her to walk through. It led her right to the end of the long corridor, where steps took her up above to the outside world once again.

She took one last look at them all and heard the Queen Ant speak above the others.

"Do this for us too, Mel. The Blue Stone will save us as well."

Mel nodded, then disappeared from sight.

Chapter 9

Although Jezebel was unusually tall, one of the things people first noticed about her was the size of her hands – they were tiny! So small, in fact, they looked quite deformed in proportion to the rest of her body. Her face however, had an odd sweetness about it. That was, until she opened her mouth. Then her whole face seemed to cave into an expression of what can only be described as supreme evil. Part of her success at ruling over so many Jebelites was down to the fact that she had a bitter sweet way of convincing people that she was right – all the time. Her smile could make you go weak at the knees while her fury could make the strongest of men grovel at her feet. No-one truly understood Jezebel, but everyone understood her rules: Do or die! No second chances – she was not to be messed with.

"So, you think you can do this?" asked Jezebel. Sam had been summoned to Jezebel's cave the next morning to discuss the plan of action.

"I know I can, M'am," came the confident reply.

"You really think you can find this imposter and bring her to me?"

"Yes, it shouldn't be difficult. I'm faster and stronger than any of your people here. In fact most of them are a little afraid of me."

Sam paused, then looking Jezebel directly in the eyes added, "M'am, just for the record, I'm afraid of nothing."

Jezebel started to smile as she continued to study Sam, a little bemused. Then, without warning, she threw her head back and laughed so loudly, Sam didn't know where to look. She seemed to be out of control, her whole body heaved, aching with laughter. For the first time in her life, Sam felt frightened.

When Jezebel finally composed herself, she turned to face Sam and in a deadly serious manner, put a few things straight.

"First, I know who is the fastest and strongest on this side of the mountain. You're looking right at her!

Secondly, you *are* afraid of something – ME!

Thirdly, don't assume anything I ask you to do is straightforward. If someone has made it to this side of the mountain without yet being caught, then they most definitely have something protecting them. This is not going to be easy. Have I made myself clear?"

Sam was speechless. Her stomach was doing somersaults and she was worried she might throw up right there in front of this ferocious bully. She nodded and accepted what Jezebel was saying, quietly reassuring herself that she was still the best person to carry this through.

"Before you can start," she continued, "I need to let you into a few secrets. The Blue Stone, as you know, is in my possession. One of the reasons I need that girl alive is that if I hold her prisoner, Wanama will be forced to call off her attempt to get The Stone. I know Wanama. She'd never let anyone she cares about come to any harm. Ha! What an idiot. I'll have her eating out of the palm of my hand, especially when I tell her what I have in store for this girl!"

Sam listened intently, impressed by the words of her leader. This was who she was striving to be like.

"But I can tell you," she went on, "that this trespasser is being guided in some way to me. To have made it halfway down the mountain means one thing."

"What's that?" asked Sam.

"Well, my dear. Much as I'd like to believe all my people are trusted followers, unfortunately that's not the case. It's clear some of the Jebelites must be helping this girl. God help them when I find out who they are. You are to trust no-one. Do you understand? No-one. Bring her straight to me, no help from anyone else, apart from my faithful flying friends." She sneered as she glanced upwards at the bats hovering above.

Jezebel spoke with such conviction, Sam found herself nodding in agreement before she had really thought about what was being asked of her.

"Once I gain the power from the precious stone, Wanama can kiss her little dream good-bye! All that I've worked for – the respect of my people, control of their minds and the exciting prospect of taking my power beyond this mountain – well..."

Jezebel's eyes glazed over as she imagined the unlimited possibilities of such a future. A world governed by her with people acting out of fear because of the almighty power of Queen Jezebel. A world filled with followers rather than leaders. Yes, this was what she had worked for all her life and no-one was going to take it away from her.

With a quick jolt back to reality, she glared at Sam.

"Get moving now! There's no time to lose and make sure you report back to me every step of the way. Go, and don't return without her!"

"Don't worry, M'am. I'll not let you down."

Sam bowed her head and walked slowly out of sight. She emerged from the cave into the dusky darkness of the mountain. Her whole expression began to change as a vague smirk appeared across her face. She rubbed her hands together and looked up. All she could see for miles ahead were monstrous trees stripped of leaves, bats as black as the night itself, swooping overhead waiting for one instruction from their leader. Sam knew this wasn't going to be easy, but she was a determined girl. She would allow nothing to prevent her from succeeding in the task before her.

There weren't many occasions when Jezebel felt afraid. However, today was one of those rare times. Her fear was mixed with an anger which she found hard to control. She never thought Wanama would dare try to get The Stone back. Thanks to Sebastian, one of her faithful Jebelites, The Stone now belonged to Jezebel. It had been unfortunate for him that his partner had fallen to his death while trying to get The Stone from Wanama's mother and that the crazy little man had managed to escape with it. However, determined to regain the respect of his leader, Sebastian did not allow this tragedy to prevent him from carrying out his duty. He had been watching close by when the weeman had delivered The Blue Stone to Wanama. He waited for the right moment to enter her house and take it,then wasted no time in getting to the top of Errigal. That was the hardest part for Sebastian, knowing he could never step over to the dark side again. His only consolation was that Jezebel could continue to use him as a spy and once she had control of both sides of the mountain, he would be generously rewarded for his good work and loyalty.

Jezebel wandered out of the cave. On the ground lay a small pile of dead leaves. She brushed them aside, revealing a tiny dark hole, only big enough for a child's hand. Rolling up her sleeves she reached down into the hole, her hand fitting just perfectly. She wiggled her fingers around until she found it. Just touching it made her feel stronger than ever. The remarkable Blue Stone of Errigal – yes, it now belonged to her!

In two more days, she pondered, when Sirius appears in the sky, it'll be me holding The Stone. And I'll be the one raising it directly in Sirius' path of light. The power released will be mine. "ALL MINE!" she shouted at the top of her voice.

As she stood up, she overheard something flying towards her. It was one of her messengers. Swooping down and landing at her feet, the bat reported the urgent message.

"I've seen her, M'am. She's made it about halfway down the mountain. There must be a force surrounding her because every time 1 try to get close to her something draws me away. We need to stop her, she's moving quickly."

"Interesting!" remarked Jezebel. "I've sent one of the Jebelites to seize her. She's smart and will hopefully use a cunning approach to capture this imbecile. Keep an eye on things and let me know if she makes it as far as my cave. I'll be ready for her. She'll not be able to depend on Wanama's power then! Go and let the others know, in case you need back-up."

Immediately, the bat took off and was out of sight as quickly as he had appeared. Jezebel watched anxiously as he vanished, then turned and walked back into her cave.

Chapter 10

Ouch! Those blasted thistle bushes are cutting the legs off me! With a deep sigh, Mel pushed her way through the prickly bushes and finally came to a halt.

Flippin' heck! How on earth am I meant to get round that?

Through the darkness she could just about make out what could only be described as a dark bottomless pit. A huge empty space loomed right in front of her and because of the growing darkness, she quickly realised it was going to be a struggle to get around it. Right. I can do this. I've come this far and I'm not giving up now! She was trying to remain positive.

Slowly she walked round the edge of the black hole, trying desperately to keep looking upwards. It was a long way down - one wrong move and she was a goner for sure. Her breathing quickened as she gingerly took one small step at a time. Every now and then she stopped to rub her eyes which were becoming more and more strained from trying to see. If I could just get over to the other side, I'd be home and dry. Surely I can't be that far from Jezebel's cave now, she reckoned.

The ants had worked tirelessly underground and taken her as far as they could. The mounds of dirt finished at the pit so Mel was sure she was very close now. The Queen Ant had instructed her to keep vigilant at all times, never forgetting to keep check overhead.

"Look out for her flying messengers," they had warned

her. "You'll know you're close when you see trees covered in bats. There'll be hundreds of them and they'll be listening carefully for any signs to indicate you're in the area."

It was becoming so dark that Mel had to feel her way carefully with each step she took, slowly, very slowly. The ground was gravelly and difficult to walk along. She continued around the gloomy abyss, eventually making it to the other side. Relieved and rather proud of herself, she muttered, That's it, not far now just a few more steps and...Suddenly her foot slid along the gravel and she fell backwards, landing with an almighty thump! "Ah..." she winced, rubbing the back of her head. In a panic she put her hand over her mouth, afraid she had disturbed the silence. Everything appeared hazy. She froze, praying she hadn't been heard by Jezebel's messengers. After a few moments she rose to her feet and took a good look around. She could hardly see a thing through the murky blackness. There were scrapes down her legs and mud stuck to her hair, but she would not give up. Mel continued on her journey, battling through the dark gloom as she tried to keep focused on what lay ahead. She reached out her arms waving them around like a maniac trying to work out where she was. Each step was further into the unknown. Deep breaths. Stay calm. Come on, concentrate. Mel was doing everything in her power to remain strong. Then just as she went to take another step she got the shock of her life. There was nothing for her to put her foot onto.

The next thing she knew, she was in mid-air!

Everything felt like it was happening in slow motion. The security of solid ground had been left behind as she fell forward into the mouth of darkness. Her yells of help echoed all around as her body tumbled over and over. Choking, gasping, she couldn't breathe. As she continued to spin out of control, the only thought in Mel's head was how would she ever retrieve The Blue Stone now?

Suddenly the darkness began to diminish. The air around her became clearer and it was getting easier to breathe again. She was slowing down, something was slowing her down! She could feel a blast of air beneath, supporting her and lifting her upwards. She was floating, somewhere within the deep pit. Filled with an overwhelming sense of calm, Mel instinctively knew something was protecting her. Sounds could be heard all around, distant voices, echoing words of comfort. It was hard to make out exactly what was being said, but one voice could be heard above all the rest,

"Keep strong, Mel. We're with you. Don't give up. Have faith in what's good. The mountain spirits are with you. You're not alone, never alone, never, never, never..." and as the voices drifted off, the falling started again. At full pelt Mel dropped deeper into the hole, eyes tightly shut as she awaited her fate.

Twisting, spinning, churning through the air and after what seemed like an eternity, but in fact what must have only been a matter of seconds, she finally landed feet first, smack on solid ground. A sharp pain shot up through both legs and Mel was sure she had broken every bone in her body!

There was nothing but rocks and darkness surrounding her. Where was she?

She didn't have to wait long to find out. Gasping as she looked ahead, she was totally stunned by what was moving towards her. Out of the darkness appeared a mass of white, skeletal figures. Hunched over and advancing towards her, they looked like they hadn't eaten for months. These were the strangest looking people she had ever seen! Gangly white bodies with long bony faces staring blankly at her. As they moved closer, she noticed that in place of their eyes, were deep empty sockets. Mel wondered if she should explain who she was and how she had arrived in this place, but somehow she didn't think they'd understand. They certainly didn't look like they were coming to offer her the hand of friendship!

"Who are you?" screamed one of them right into her face.

Terrified, Mel swallowed hard and pretended not to be intimidated by these creatures.

"I honestly don't know what happened. I was walking round the mouth of the hole and..."

"Shut it!" yelled another one. "You're lying!" And with that several of them shuffled over and prodded her in the back. "Move! You're coming with us."

"Ouch! That hurts!"

Mel soon realised why it hurt her so much. Each one of their hands was bent into a bony fist. These people didn't appear to have any fingers. Chuckles came from the others and their laughter grew louder and louder as more joined in, mocking her words.

The pushing and shoving continued and finally Mel

could take no more of it.

"Look, will you please stop it. I'm capable of walking myself you know!" Her fear had been overtaken by annoyance at how they were treating her.

"Well, well. We've got a smart one here, less talking and more walking. Come on, move!"

"Can't you for heaven's sake show some manners! You lot should be ashamed of yourselves. You're nothing but a pack of bullies! Now if you just show me where you want me to go I'll follow, ok?"

Everyone stood still in amazement at the boldness of this girl. Somehow it didn't feel right to keep pushing her around. It didn't seem like she was here to create trouble, so she was simply led to a long dark tunnel and told to stay there until they had decided what to do with her.

Mel crouched into a corner and tried not to let her surroundings upset her too much. It was dark and cold. She felt a million miles from home.

Chapter 11

After some time of being left alone in the dark tunnel, Mel became aware of someone standing beside her. Startled, she stood up, cowering into the wall for support.

"Try not to feel afraid. We're harmless, really. I know this whole thing must be an awful shock to you, but believe me, you are one of the lucky ones."

She couldn't believe what he'd just said.

"What are you on about? Have you any idea how important it is for me to get out of here? I can't stay, not a moment longer. Please help me to get away, please, I'm begging you."

Mel's eyes filled with tears and she turned away so the stranger couldn't see. She hated anyone seeing her cry. But the tears just spilled onto her face until, before she knew it, she was sobbing uncontrollably.

"Come here," said the man tenderly. "It's not as bad as you think. Look, we have no choice but to stay here. We can't escape, thanks to that heartless, cruel dragon. She's made sure of that." He turned away and paused, reflecting on the horror of his unbearable ordeal.

"She's destroyed my life," he continued. "I'm stuck here forever, with no means of escape and look at me! Even if I could escape, my appearance would terrify people. We all look like the walking dead and believe me, we may as well be."

Mel felt sorry for the man. She could tell there was something tender and genuine about him. He was trying hard to keep command of his emotions. Moving forward, she rested her hand on his bony shoulder, undisturbed by his strange appearance.

"Who did this to you?" she asked, although she had already guessed.

"Who do you think? That beast of a woman Jezebel. This is her way of punishing us if we don't obey her rules or, in my case, show any signs of weakness. Thanks to her, my life is over, finished!"

"But why don't you try to escape?" Mel was confused. "There's so many of you. Surely you could all get together and work something out. Anything would be better than spending the rest of your days in this place!"

"We can't. Look!" He held his hands straight out in front of him so that Mel could see them clearly. She had already noticed these people had no fingers, but wasn't quite sure what he was getting at.

"She wanted to make sure we would never be able to get out of here, so this was part of her clever plan. She removed the only tools we had to enable us to escape – our fingers! You see, the only way out of this deep pit is to climb our way out, but try climbing when your hand's in the shape of a fist. It's impossible! That's why everyone in here feels so angry and frustrated all the time. It's like living in limbo."

Mel was speechless. She couldn't believe the extent of Jezebel's cruelty. This woman was truly evil, to inflict this torture on these poor people.

"But you," continued the man, "you could get out of here. Your hands haven't closed over like ours. She mustn't have any idea you're here. My advice to you is to escape before word gets back to her."

Looking upwards into the pitch black, Mel didn't honestly believe there was any way she could make it back up.

Meanwhile, the others were holding a meeting to decide what to do with the girl. Some were afraid she'd been sent by Jezebel as a spy, but this was soon dismissed when they realised how frightened she was.

"We can't just leave her here," said another. "She's not like us. She'll never fit in. She has human requirements like food and water. We can't provide that."

Everyone listened and thought about what to do next. No-one was prepared for an outsider joining their sombre world.

Suddenly a voice broke the silence.

"Hang on! This girl might be able to help us."

"How on earth could she help us?" demanded Groggin, one of the older members of the group.

"Look, if we could just convince her to climb up the side and mould little shelves into the side of the pit, this would mean we could rest our arms onto something while pulling ourselves up. We don't need our fingers for grip."

The others stood still, contemplating the idea.

"She would be in front of us doing all the work," he continued.

"We would just have to follow behind using the shelves as arm rests and with quick heaves pull our way to the top. This could really work!"

For the first time in what felt like ages people began to feel some hope. Smiles spread over their faces and within seconds everyone was talking at once. It could be done. The stranger had been sent from above to save them. This was an opportunity they couldn't let slip away.

Mel had started to tell the man all about The Blue Stone and how she had been chosen to rescue it from Jezebel. As he listened, his expression started to change. The young man looked like he'd just seen a ghost.

Mel however, continued, interested to find out what his life had been like before all of this had happened.

But he had become distant and Mel wasn't sure whether to continue with her questions.

"What did you do to end up here?" she asked, reluctantly.

He turned away from her gaze.

"Tell me," begged Mel. "What made that monster send you here, away from your family?"

"I let her know that I wasn't sure if I could complete one of her tasks," he muttered quietly.

"What did she ask you to do?"

He paused for a moment before replying.

"She asked me to get rid of someone who'd made it over to this side of the mountain. An imposter, I think was how she put it."

They looked directly at each other and both knew what the other was thinking. Mel was the reason he was here. If it hadn't been for her this man wouldn't be where he was today.

"Oh no. I'm so sorry," she whispered, unable to look at him.

He took a step towards her and gently placed his fist on her shoulder.

"Look, don't get upset. None of this is your fault. The only person to blame is Jezebel. You are the one who can stop all this. You must put an end to her power. Don't give up now."

Mel bit her lip till it turned purple. She knew what she had to do.

"I'm going to do it. I'm going to climb out of here should it kill me!"

The man smiled.

"By the way, what's your name?" she asked.

" Zurin," came the reply.

Chapter 12

Mel was ready to help Zurin and the others escape. It didn't take long for her to realise they were harmless and their initial unfriendly manner was due to their desperate plight.

After their conversation, Zurin had brought Mel to the others to give her a chance to explain why she was there. They put their escape plan to her. When she told them about how she needed to get The Blue Stone back to Wanama before midnight tomorrow, the exact time when Sirius would cast its light directly above the summit of Errigal, she was bombarded with many questions. Everyone was anxious to know what Wanama's plan was and how Mel thought she could possibly make it to Jezebel's cave without getting caught.

"You're going to need our help as well, you know," said Groggin, who had been one of the ones who had initially pushed Mel around.

"I think it's important for us to get out of here as quickly as possible before she's onto you and then we can help you get to Jezebel's cave. How does that sound?"

Everyone nodded in agreement, including Mel.

"We'll line up in order of weakest first. That way, if anyone slips or misplaces their footing, there are others behind to help push each other up. Does everyone understand what to do?"

Groggin had taken on the role of leader. Although not the cleverest of the bunch, he was a natural organiser. It was he who had come up with the idea of the escape plan.

"Now, listen up. This is probably the only chance we're going to have to get out of this place. Let's not waste it. Everyone has to stay focused and try to remain calm. You arc cach responsible for the person ahead. If you see any sign of the person in front slipping, put your fist under their foot and push as hard as you can. Everyone ok with that?"

A sea of white heads bobbed up and down in response. It felt good to have someone take control. Groggin had the gift of making people believe in themselves, giving them hope when they needed it.

He turned to face Mel, who had remained very quiet throughout his talk.

"Are you alright? I know it's going to be difficult Mel, but you can do this."

Mel looked into the crowd of these poor lost souls. They had had everything strippcd from them. The last thing she wanted to do was to discourage them now. They were all so full of hope and she was the only one who could make it happen for them. Mel straightened herself up and addressed the group.

"Of course I can do this. Look how far I've come from the other side of Errigal. I'm not stopping now. Not till I've completed what I've come here to do. We're a team. We'll get out of here. I promise."

Her assurance was all they needed. Each of the figures started stamping their feet on the ground as a sign of approval.

"Right, get into line. Mel, you up front. We can't hang about. It's only a matter of time before Jezebel finds out where you are. Come on, let's get going."

Mel stood at the front of the long line of white figures. She took a look behind at all the faces with mixed expressions of both excitement and fear.

Where was Zurin? She wanted to give him a hug before she set off. He'd been so good to her and after all, it was because of her that he was here in the first place. She searched frantically through the crowd.

"Come on, we need to get moving," pleaded Groggin.

Mel ignored his pleas. She had to find Zurin and make sure he was going to get out safely with all the others.

"Zurin, where are you?" she yelled.

Everyone turned around and tried to help locate him, but he wasn't there.

"Look, we're running out of time," said Groggin impatiently. "If Zurin has chosen not to come, then that's up to him. Now come on, Mel. No-one's going to make it if we don't leave now."

"No! I'm not going without him." She turned and darted back towards the tunnel.

Running as fast as she could, she hoped beyond hope that she would find him. He was one of the main reasons she was so determined to lead this escape. He had to be reunited with his family.

Finally, she reached the opening of the tunnel. Her instincts were right. There he was, huddled in a corner, shivering and petrified. He turned his head away in shame.

"Go away!" he begged. "Just get out of here and leave me alone. Go on, the others need you."

She could tell he was crying. Mel had never felt so sorry for anyone in her whole life. He was so frightened. How was she going to convince him to come with her?

She walked over and knelt down beside him.

"Zurin," she said quietly. "A few days ago I was chased by a girl who was way bigger than me. She was scary in every way. The boys in the village were even afraid of her. And here she was chasing me. I knew if I was caught I was getting it big time. I honestly thought at one stage she was going to kill me. I ran like I've never run before. I kept running, even though my legs felt numb. The furthest I'd ever run before that was to the sweet shop at the top of my street. But something kept me going, even though I was scared. I seemed to get a strength from somewhere. I never believed I could do it, but eventually I burned her out and got away. If anyone had told me beforehand that I could've outrun her I'd never have believed them. Sometimes fear's not a bad thing Zurin, sometimes it's what we need to make us stronger."

Her voice trailed off as she was sure Zurin was beyond listening.

But, he turned to face her. He could see she meant every word.

"I'm such a coward," he whimpered. "All my life I've tried to do things that would make people proud of me, but I always end up letting them down. I'm pathetic. It's by my own weakness that I ended up here! You're different from me. You're determined. You're not easily put off. It's better if I stay here. I'd be no help to the others."

"Come on, Zurin. You can't mean that. You'd be left here on your own, think how scary that would be. What's the worst that can happen? We don't make it. Well then, you're no worse off than when you started. Listen, I'm not leaving without you, so make your mind up. We either stay here and wait for Jezebel to find us, or we try to find her and get The Blue Stone back to where it belongs. Remember, you're the main reason I agreed to this escape plan in the first place."

While Zurin was trying to reconcile everything Mel had been saying, shouts could be heard in the distance.

"They need us. Please, Zurin. They're desperate to get out of here. Do it for them."

She reached out her hand and carefully took his fist, helping him up to his feet. He followed her to the opening of the tunnel, then stopped.

"I want to do this. There's nothing I want more than to see my family again."

"Come on," she continued reassuringly. "I'll be ahead carving the way for you. You've no need to worry."

The two of them walked back to where everyone was waiting. No-one asked any questions, there was no time. There was a quiet understanding among everyone and that was enough.

"Right, we're ready for action," beamed Mel. "Ready?"

Yells of agreement boomed throughout and just before Mel made her first move, she took a quick look behind to make sure Zurin was alright.

There he was at the back of the line, waiting nervously to take his turn. She threw him a smile, took a deep breath as she glanced upwards and began the climb.

Chapter 13

One of the wild boars which lived in the forest stepped out to give some important news to Sam. "Mel has fallen to her death." He faced the deep pit a few feet away. "We heard her screams and came racing out in time to see her disappear."

This wasn't good, as Sam was desperate to prove to Jezebel that she could complete the task. Her leader had insisted that she wanted Mel alive. Now that she had fallen hundreds of feet below, this was going to be impossible!

"Thanks for letting me know. Say nothing in the meantime."

The boar lowered his head and made his way back into the forest where he and the others could keep a watch on things in case they were needed.

Stepping into Jezebel's world had changed Sam's life forever. She thought about that fateful day when she had chased Mel through the town, convinced she would catch her. When Mel outran her, she couldn't face going back to the others in the town and have them laugh at how she had allowed Mel to get away. That's when she decided to stay on Errigal. Only, unlike Mel, she had ventured to the dark side of the mountain, walking into Jezebel's world. This was where she felt she belonged.

Slowly she made her way towards the black pit, not really sure what to expect. Poised at the edge, she couldn't help thinking about how frightened Mel must have felt as she lost her footing and fell. A smile appeared over Sam's face.

Serves her right, she got what she deserved! Only problem is, how am I going to look in front of Jezebel? I don't want Jezebel thinking I didn't have the courage to complete my search for Mel.

She walked forwards and backwards for a few moments trying to work out what she'd say to Jezebel. The only thing she could think of was to tell Jezebel that she had had to push Mel into the pit. Yes, she could say there was a strong force surrounding her and it was the only way. That way she'd look like she'd done all she could and not lose respect from her leader.

"You finally got what you deserved!" she bellowed, looking down into the pit.

As her voice echoed, she thought she could hear some sounds coming from below. Surely not. Not here, in a dark empty pit. There it was again. What on earth was it? Gradually, moans could be heard and then the sound of falling gravel. Next she could hear voices, lots of them. What was going on?

Sam bent forward, trying to get a better view. She could make out the top of someone's head, long hair and arms outstretched, clambering to get to the top. This was unbelievable! How anyone could make it out of this pit was nothing short of a miracle. Sam could see there were others following, each shouting instructions to the person behind. How many are there, wondered Sam, as she kept staring downwards in disbelief.

However, nothing could have prepared Sam for what happened next. Two hands appeared, gripping onto the edge. With one final heave, Mel had made it. Lifting her head, she got the shock of her life. She recognised this person standing in front of her. It was the boygirl who had viciously chased her through the town first leading her to the base of Errigal. Mel couldn't disguise the terror that filled her eyes as she stood face to face with Sam who was glaring straight at her.

"You! What are you doing here?" she asked, bewildered.

"Well you see, you little idiot, some of us round here have more sense than others. Unlike you and all your weakling friends, I work for the most powerful person on Errigal!"

A heavy silence lingered over both of them until Mel suddenly remembered there was an army of people coming up behind her. Quickly she spun round and turned her thoughts to getting everyone safely to the surface.

"Come on!" she yelled frantically, making sure no-one lost their footing. "Reach for my hand!"

One by one she managed to heave each one back into the world they had once known.

Sam stood watching, delighted by the opportunity which was unfolding before her. It wouldn't be long before the bats returned. Then this little gathering would be history! A bonus for Jezebel to not only have Mel as prisoner but also all these fools who thought they could escape and get away with it.

Mel was overcome with relief when she caught sight of Zurin, clambering up the side of the pit. Anxiety and fear were written all over his face as he came into view.

"That's it, you're nearly there. Come on Zurin, reach up..."

Her heart was pounding as she took hold of Zurin's

arm. Don't let go, she kept repeating to herself. Finally, with one last haul, he reached solid ground. Looking around him in disbelief, he shook his head then walked over to Mel throwing his arms around her.

"You've saved my life. I will be forever grateful to you."

Just then, Sam intervened. "Ok. Party's over! Break it up," she sneered as she yanked Zurin out of Mel's reach.

Swaggering over to Mel, she met her eye to eye. "Right YOU! You're coming with me."

Gripped with fear, Mel swallowed hard and mustered up all her strength.

"Get lost! I wouldn't go with you if you were the last person on earth!"

Mel pulled away from Sam and went back over to join the others. But Sam had other plans. As she looked upwards she could see the sky had suddenly darkened as it filled with hundreds of bats descending towards them.

"Wonderful," she murmured.

"Run!" yelled Mel. "Find cover somewhere, anywhere."

At once everyone scrambled in different directions in search of anything that would shield them from the creatures which were now circling above.

Mel began to run with the others but didn't get very far before she felt something grab her hair so forcefully it made her fall to the ground.

"Get up!" pleaded Zurin. "Come on, Mel. Get up for heaven's sake!"

But it was too late. Sam had used her foot to pin her to the ground. She had let her get away once before. Not this time.

"Go on, Zurin," sobbed Mel. "I can't move. Don't stop now!"

Zurin stood for a moment looking back at the girl who had shown him nothing but kindness and courage.

"Mel," he muffled through his tears, accepting defeat as he disappeared out of her view.

Chapter 14

"What are we going to do?" pleaded Zurin. Groggin looked at his friend, unable to give him an answer.

"She'll kill Mel if we don't do something fast!" continued Zurin. Shaking his head, he desperately tried to think of some way of rescuing her.

"Pssst! Over here!" Someone was lurking opposite them in the darkness.

Groggin looked round to see where the voice was coming from. Zurin could just about make out a tiny figure crouched behind one of the trees. He was signalling for them to come over.

"Wait, it could be a trap!" Groggin was taking no chances.

"Come on," said Zurin. "He wants to tell us something."

They shuffled across to the tree, desperate to stay hidden from the bats which were hovering close by.

When they made it safely across, the stranger appeared from behind the tree. Both men were surprised to see that standing in front of them was a child no more than ten years old. He looked like he was camouflaged to blend in with the landscape. When he spoke, both men knew this boy was smart.

"Come with me," he instructed. "I know where she's hidden The Stone. I can lead you straight to it."

"Really?" Groggin had to be sure he wasn't leading them on.

"Quickly," he whispered. "It's not far from here. Follow me."

Suddenly Zurin stopped in his tracks. Tugging at Groggin, he pulled him closer and could hardly get the words out. " I recognise that voice! Groggin, I know the boy...it's my son, Mathieu!"

"What? Are you sure?" Groggin was practically miming the words so the boy wouldn't hear.

"Yes, I'm sure. It's definitely him." Zurin tried hard not to let his emotions take over. To be seen like this by his son was painful.

"Keep up!" The boy was running ahead like a wild animal, desperate to lead the men to The Stone.

Running behind, Groggin grabbed Zurin's arm.

"Look, I know this is hard, but you can't let him know who you are. He clearly doesn't recognise you. There's too much at stake here and we could end up losing everything."

Difficult as it was, Zurin nodded in agreement. He knew Groggin was right. Thanks to Jezebel he looked like a freakish skeletal figure. How would he ever guess this was his dad? In some ways it made it easier to stay focused. He had to do whatever he could to get The Stone, even if it meant hiding the truth from his son for the time being. Suddenly, the young boy stopped in his tracks.

"There. She keeps it over there," he said, pointing to a mound of leaves on the ground. "She'll be out any minute to check on it."

"How can you be so sure?" inquired Groggin. Zurin remained quietly in the background.

"Just wait and see. She comes out at this time every

day just to hold it. I've been watching her, waiting to get my revenge for what she's done to me and my family."

He spoke these words through clenched teeth. Zurin could hardly contain himself. He wanted to rush over to his son to reassure him he was still alive. But a cold glare from Groggin reminded him this wasn't the right time.

Right on cue she appeared. The men watched in amazement as she reached into the ground and lifted out The Stone. She smiled as she gently caressed it.

"See, what did I tell you?" hissed the young boy. "This is your chance to take it."

"Ah, my sweet little gem, encasing all that power just for me. All for me." She let out a muffled laugh. It gave Jezebel such pleasure to hold The Stone. She carefully placed it back in its hiding place and returned to her cave.

"Right!" whispered Zurin to Groggin. " You wait here and keep lookout while I see if I can get it." Zurin turned to thank Matthieu but he had disappeared back into the darkness of the forest. He felt he'd just been stabbed through the heart. He looked at Groggin expecting some words of encouragement, but Groggin was beginning to feel afraid of what they were about to get into.

"This is madness Zurin. She's bound to have people watching."

For a moment he wondered if his friend was right, then he remembered what Mel had told him in the death pit before they had made their escape - fear can make us stronger.

Ignoring Groggin's words, he threw a reassuring smile towards his companion. " Ok, wish me luck."

"Careful," said Groggin tenderly, feeling a mixture of anger and admiration for this man. "You'll only get one chance at this."

Cautiously, he took one step forward. The cave was surrounded by trees, all bent forward as if bowing to their leader. He crouched down and ran as fast as he could to the first tree in sight. Standing for a moment, he planned his next move. There were enough trees around to allow him to get closer without being seen. Swiftly he wove in and out of the trees until he was just a stone's throw from the jackpot! It was then he realised his problem– he wouldn't be able to lift The Stone out. How could he pick it up without using his fingers? Looking down at his hands shaped like fists, he felt defeated .The hole in which The Stone was buried was tiny!

Groggin immediately knew something was wrong. He couldn't understand why Zurin wasn't moving any further... he was so close now. Time was running out. It wouldn't be long before the bats would be overhead, eager to tell their mistress all that had happened.

Matthieu was keeping guard, watching for Jebelites. He glanced towards Zurin. Why was he just standing there? He couldn't understand what was going on. He scrambled across and within seconds was by Zurin's side.

"What's up?"

"Look!" Zurin held his fists out for Matthieu to see.

"How can I possibly get The Stone? Even if I had my hands, the hole's too small. They would never fit."

He was right. Without wasting another minute, Matthieu knelt by the hole and squeezing his hand tightly, forced it down as hard as he could. His hand scraped through the gravel as he searched frantically with his fingers. His hand ached with the pressure from the small opening, but despite this he kept pushing further down until he felt something.

There it is, he said to himself feeling its smooth round shape. He gripped it firmly and glanced up at Zurin.

"Got it!" he mouthed.

Zurin turned towards Groggin and nodded.

"Come on!" muttered Groggin as he looked on, becoming more and more anxious as each second passed.

With a final tug, Matthieu managed to pull his hand out, clenching The Blue Stone with every fibre of his being.

"There it is!" He smiled as he held it out for Zurin to look at.

"Wow!" A shimmery blue light radiated from The Stone. It was startling. For a moment Matthieu just froze. He couldn't believe he was standing there, holding something which contained such power.

"Let's go!" urged Zurin, realising time was quickly running out. "We need to get The Stone to Mel."

Matthieu heaped the pile of leaves back over the hole and followed Zurin as they hurried over to Groggin.

Without a word, he held out The Stone for Groggin to see.

Looks of amazement were exchanged between the three, then, they all took off, disappearing into the forest from where they had come.

"So, this is it!" Sam spat into Mel's face, bruised and cut from the thistles Sam had dragged her through. Here they were again at the edge of the pit. She booted her in the back of her legs. Mel dropped to the ground and lay for a moment before getting back up again, but just as she managed to straighten herself up, Sam punched her in the stomach, causing Mel to double up and fall to her knees.

"Let me go! I'm nothing to you!" Mel screamed through her tears.

"You're pathetic. Can't you see, there's no escape. Why would I let you go now?"

Sam dragged Mel over to the edge of the pit by the hair. Whimpering, Mel was trying desperately not to let Sam know how painful this was. In the middle of it all she thought she could hear sounds in the distance. It sounded like heavy stamping which was becoming increasingly louder.

"What's this?" Sam stared at the sight before her. An army of skeletal figures were walking towards her. It was now their turn to do something for Mel.

"Get away from me you fools! Jezebel will never let you away with this."

Sam started to back away, but the wave of white creatures continued to move speedily in her direction. Sam knew she had to do something fast. She looked around searching for something to fend off her attackers. All around lay gravel and rocks. That might do it. Lifting a handful of stones she fired them at the frontrunners. Quickly they raised their fists to try to protect their eyes. But, as Sam had cleverly worked out, having fists instead of hands meant they were unable to pick up stones to retaliate.

"Great!" smiled Sam. "This just might work!"

One by one they began to retreat as Sam continued pelting them.

However, she hadn't noticed Mel was now on her feet. As she struggled to stand, she lifted the largest rock she could find and fired it straight at Sam. It hit her right in the middle of her forehead, causing her to fall to the ground.

"Run!" yelled Mel to the others. "Get out of here, quick!"

Everyone scattered towards the forest, leaving Mel to decide on the next plan of action. Suddenly a herd of wild boar appeared at the edge of the forest. Their nostrils flared to show they were about to attack. Mel stood very still, trying to outstare them. A couple of them took a few steps forward with the others following close behind. Then, without warning they charged towards her, grunting loudly as they drew nearer. Mel knew she was in serious trouble. She took to her heels and tried to run for cover even though she could hardly see ahead through the darkness. One of the boar managed to catch up with her digging his teeth into her ankles and causing her to fall to the ground. The rest quickly surrounded her so she couldn't escape.

Immediately there was a great surge of wings as hundreds of bats swooped down from the trees towards their victim. Mel covered her head and closed her eyes. This was it. It was over. She had nowhere to run to. One by one she could feel the bats landing on her. She couldn't breathe as they tried to smother her. As their wings beat against her body, she felt like she was being whipped a million times. When would this stop?

Slipping into unconsciousness, she suddenly became aware of a gleaming light. It was blinding. She tried to open her eyes but it was too bright. She screwed her eyes to try to see where she was. Is this what it felt like to die?

Before she knew it, hundreds of bats took to the skies, panicking. The wild boar were screeching as they turned round and ran back into the forest. The light was startling, too much for them to take.

Miraculously the light filled Mel with strength and warmth. Everywhere appeared blue, a beautiful deep sapphire blue...

As the light faded she saw the outline of two people she recognised. Standing in front of her were Zurin and Groggin.

"Zurin, is that you?" Mel wasn't sure if she was dreaming.

"Yes it's me. And look what I've brought you."

Zurin was holding The Stone tightly between his two fists. He stepped over to Mel and without a word released The Stone into her hands. The light glowed again, but this time it radiated around both men. The light travelled through them giving both of them renewed strength. Their arms felt tingly and started to shake. No-one really knew what was happening. Then, as quickly as the light had intensified, so it faded once again. Zurin looked down and couldn't believe his eyes.

"My hands! Look!"

Groggin was speechless. He had his arms outstretched and was wriggling his fingers in utter disbelief.

"We've got our hands back! Oh my word...." Groggin stared at Zurin. "Look at you." Zurin looked at his arms and legs.

"This is a miracle," he whispered. Slowly Groggin's body took on a similar transformation. Both men had regained their normal shape.

"Wow!" muttered Groggin finding it hard to take in. Instinctively he reached his hand out to his friend, who did the same. To be able to use their hands again felt wonderful. It was a handshake neither would ever forget.

"Are you ok, Mel?" asked Zurin bending down to help her. Mel couldn't speak. She couldn't believe the transformation which had just occurred in her two friends.

"You look so different," she said shaking her head in disbelief. "Zurin, I can't believe you managed to get it! How did you do it?"

"With some help, but no time for explanations right now."

She limped over to her two friends and gave them both a hug.

"How can I ever thank you?"

Zurin hung his head, slightly embarrassed, but proud he'd been able to help. At last he felt he'd done something which had required courage.

"Right, let's stay focused," continued Mel. "We've very little time. We need to get back up the mountain at top speed. Somehow we must get word to Wanama that we have The Stone and she needs to be at the top of the mountain, ready to take it from us. Time's running out."

"What about our families?" asked Groggin. "They're in serious danger. Jezebel must know by now what's happened. We can't leave them."

"If we don't get this to Wanama, everyone's ruined for good! I need one of you to come with me. Someone needs to get a message telling her to be at the top of the mountain, ready to take The Stone."

After a short pause Zurin spoke up.

"Go on Groggin. I'll go with Mel. You get the others to safety. Hurry!"

Groggin didn't need any more time.

"Good luck, both of you. We'll be here waiting."

"Let's go," urged Mel as she clasped The Stone tightly.

Encased in gleaming light, the two took off, making their way up the mountain, unsure if they would make it in time.

Chapter 15

A stream of light shone along the river outside Wanama's house. If you looked closely beneath the surface of the water, you could see hundreds of rainbow fish darting to and fro between the rocks. Occasionally one, in an attempt to show off to the others, would leap up, spin round in mid air then boldly dive back in again. Quite a spectacle! Anyone watching this couldn't be blamed for thinking life was simply perfect on this side of the mountain.

Inside her house, Wanama was beginning to feel concerned. She should have heard something by now. What if Mel was lying hurt, too frightened to get help? Worse still, if she had been captured by Jezebel. There was no knowing what that beast of a woman would do to her! Her thoughts filled her with fear. *I shouldn't have let her go. She's not familiar with Jezebel's territory. Heavens... it's too late now. How will I ever forgive myself if something's happened to Mel?*

Unable to stand it any longer, she darted out of her house, making a high-pitched whistling sound to gather the animals together. Straight away creatures appeared from all parts, moving hastily in her direction. Wanama waited for complete silence, then spoke.

"I'm worried. Something's wrong." She looked up towards the top of Errigal, then continued.

"Mel should've returned by now. I was hoping it wouldn't come to this, but we've no choice. We've got to intervene."

Quickly she went into action, drawing the animals together in groups.

"You lot," she said addressing the meerkats. "I need you to get a message to the ants across the other side of Errigal. They're going to have to send out a search party for Mel. This will have to be done underground, otherwise you'll get caught. "

Theo took charge. He raised his tail as a sign he understood what was to be done, then hissed in the faces of the other meerkats to establish his authority for the task which lay ahead.

"Ok. Next, I need as many of you as possible to swim upstream to the top of the mountain," she instructed, turning to the rainbow fish. "It'll be a tough climb, but you need to be there so our messengers on the dark side can get news back to us as quickly as possible."

"Leave it to us," the fish chorused as they plunged out of sight.

At the edge of the river, just at the opening of the forest, twelve antelope stood patiently, waiting to be told what they could do. Wanama looked across in their direction. These creatures were strong. They had antlers, twice the size of their heads – firm, pointed, potentially good weapons if things turned nasty. She swallowed hard before speaking to them, for what she was about to ask was one of the most difficult things she would ever do. Although they had the appearance of being strong and mighty, in truth, they were the most gentle animals you could ever meet. She turned to face them.

"It's likely since we've heard nothing, that Mel's been

taken captive. Now, listen carefully. You need to cross over into the darkness of Errigal. Your duty is to rescue Mel. To do this, you must wait for the ants to tell you where to go. They will know her exact whereabouts. Wait at the top and don't start your attack until you are instructed. Trust no-one. Jezebel has spies all over the place."

"You know what this means," she continued. "I'm sorry, but you're the only hope we have of fighting against Jezebel to get this girl and The Stone back."

Trying to remain composed, she carried on.

"Mel is the only one who can survive on both sides of Errigal. She is our only hope of ever stopping Jezebel from gaining complete control. It's our duty to ensure her safety."

A stony silence lingered in the warm air. Several of the antelope walked over to the edge of the river and took a long slow drink. Wanama watched intently and couldn't help thinking of the many times they had wandered down from the forest to drink from their favourite spot, always finding time to stop and talk with her. They had had so many wonderful conversations over the years and there had never been any doubt how much they appreciated their freedom on Errigal– on this side of Errigal.

The realisation that this was soon to end was nearly too much to take in. Wanama had just asked them to do something which they never thought they would have to do– step across the summit of Errigal into the darkness of Jezbel's world. Once this happened, they could never return.

"Is this what you really want from us?"

Brazier, the leader of the group gracefully stepped forward.

Without a word and barely looking in their direction, Wanama nodded.

Brazier returned to the others and one by one the antelope slowly walked towards Wanama. As each one approached her, they stopped, bowed their head in respect and went on their way. Wanama smiled as they walked past, though her eyes were filled with tears. They possessed such dignity, even at a time like this. On their approach, she stepped forward and stroked their antlers as a mother would a child. She watched the herd until the last of them finally disappeared from sight.

"Wait up, Zurin!" yelled Mel. She was amazed at how quickly he could move. Zurin looked round and shouted back, "Hurry up, time's running out!"

Mel knew they had to move fast. She'd already managed to get a message to the ants telling them to let Wanama know she was on her way. Hopefully they would act quickly and Wanama would be waiting at the top.

Clambering over the rough ground, they were able to use the light from The Stone as a guide to help them see where they were going. Everywhere around them was pitch black.

"I don't think it's too far now," said Mel, certain the ground had become a little easier to walk upon.

"Yes, I knew it!" She'd spotted the thistle bushes she had battled through at the beginning of her journey.

"We're nearly there, Zurin," she gasped. "We've made it!"

Zurin held his hand out to Mel, partly to help her with the final stretch of the climb but more as a sign of friendship. Her spirit was unbreakable.

"Thanks," she said smiling. He returned her smile, but a couple of moments later his expression changed to fear. Mel could see something was wrong but couldn't make out what exactly was happening.

"Zurin, you ok?" she whispered. The next thing she heard a yelp from her friend and saw that he'd been yanked backwards by something. He was struggling. Mel didn't take time to find out how many others were there. Impulsively, she leapt forward to try to free her companion. Holding The Blue Stone tightly in her hand, she pushed and shoved her way to try to get to Zurin, but there were too many. If only she could see what was going on. It was so dark.

Maybe if I use some of the light from The Stone, I might be able to see, she thought.

As the light glowed between her fingers, she could make out several large, black figures. Towering over the little man, they continually beat him till he couldn't take anymore. Mel couldn't believe her eyes.

"ZURIN!" she screamed. "Zurin! No, get off him! Get away from him!"

The tall figures turned towards Mel.

"Hand over The Stone. You know you could make this a lot easier on yourself if you do."

Although she couldn't see where the voice was coming from, it didn't put her off.

"There's no way you're ever getting The Stone!"

Her attention turned to Zurin lying helpless on the ground.

"What have you done to him? He means nothing to you!"

She tried to make her way over to him, but someone grabbed her arm and pushed her to the ground.

"I said, hand over The Stone. It belongs to us."

Mel lay for a moment face down, looking towards the ground. She could hear one of them walking towards her. This was her chance. Waiting until he was right up beside her, she twisted round and booted him in the leg as hard as she could.

"Ahhhhhh, you vicious little..."

She didn't wait a moment longer and jumped to her feet, knowing she had to get to the top of Errigal to hand over The Stone before they got it off her.

Running as fast as she could, Mel didn't look back.

"Keep looking ahead," she repeated over and over again. The Stone was still in her hands, lighting up the way for her.

Mel could hear people behind her. She knew they wouldn't stop at anything. Her legs kept going, even though she felt like she was going to collapse!

Suddenly she could see it. The summit of Errigal was in sight! Glimmers of light shone from the other side. All she had to do was cross over and she was home and dry.

"Up here!" came a yell from the top.

Mel looked up and saw the oddest looking man reaching out his hands to her. He was standing on the other side. As she drew closer she worked out who it was. It was the weeman. She recognised him from Wanama's description when she told Mel about how he had first delivered The Stone to her.

"Give it here, quick. Pass it to me. Hurry! They're right behind you."

Mel quickly charged to the top trying to resist looking round to see how close the others were. She placed The Stone in the weeman's hands. Just as she released it, she felt something tangled in her hair. It was moving, flapping against the back of her head. Brushing her fingers through her hair she knew straight away what it was. The bats were swooping down in droves. The little demons clamped their teeth on the ends of her hair and yanked as hard as they could. Mel tried to fight back, but there were just too many of them.

As she lay helpless, a loud rumble came from beneath. It grew so loud, it became deafening. Part of the ground began to rise up like a huge mound, then without any warning, exploded, spraying stones and dirt all over the place. Everyone was covered and could barely see for the grit in their eyes. After a few moments, when the dirt had settled, millions of ants emerged from the ground. They were everywhere. Each one of them looked like they were on some kind of special mission. They worked quickly and harmoniously, crawling up each person's leg. It only took a matter of seconds before they had completely covered the Jebelites. Screams of terror could be heard at first and then they became muffled sounds as the ants crawled into their mouths and up their noses. Mel stood, transfixed. She was the only one left untouched. Her eyes searched frantically for Zurin, but he was nowhere to be seen.

"STOP!" yelled Mel. "We need to get to Jezebel before she gets to the other Jebelites. Zurin and Groggin's families and many others are in danger. They're going to need our help."

Instantly, more ants appeared.

"We can try, but she's quicker than us. I don't think we can make that kind of ground."

"The antelope. Get them, they're at the top waiting to attack!" yelled one of the ants.

Quickly they scurried up to the summit and in no time a herd of antelope were making their way down. One of them charged over to Mel.

"Get to the top, now!" he instructed. "Wanama's waiting for you. Leave the rest to us. We'll see to Jezebel. Don't worry. We'll make sure your friends are safe."

Mel ran at top speed, past the remains of the Jebelites. Could tiny ants really cause that kind of destruction?

Up towards the top, she could make out the figure of a person standing, the sun shining against her back. It was Wanama. Without a second thought, she ran as fast as she could, straight into her arms.

"Where is it?" asked Wanama urgently.

"I handed it over to the weeman. He was waiting for me at the top."

"Where did he go?" asked Wanama, curious that he always seemed to turn up at the right times.

Suddenly a familiar voice could be heard.

"Hey Wanama, we've got it! The Blue Stone, it's safe, in our hands again."

Wanama spun round to see the weeman jumping up and down with excitement.

"We got it and better still, Jezebel has been captured by her own people. Can you believe it? The Jebelites have turned against their leader. Remarkable! You can call off the chase. Everything is under control."

This was truly unbelievable! Wanama was sure she had misheard him.

"It's lucky for us I have people working for me on Jezebel's side of the mountain. Call them spies, imposters, whatever you like. Anyway, they ambushed Jezebel on the way down. There were so many of them that not even the bats could put up a good enough fight."

Wanama took a deep breath and held Mel's face in her hands.

"We did it, my dear. I knew we'd get it back. Thank you."

Her whole face lit up with the most wonderful warm smile. Knowing time was precious, she whistled as loudly as she could and instantly the meerkats, rainbow fish and birds of all shapes and sizes appeared from nowhere.

"Call off the chase immediately. We have The Stone. Tell the antelope their work is done. We need them all at the top of Errigal right now. We've less than an hour before Sirius appears. Quick, go on. There's no time to lose!"

Chapter 16

The weeman had told Wanama and Mel to wait back at the house and he would bring The Stone to them. He assured them he had hidden it carefully so there would be no danger of anyone trying to get it off him when he went to the top of Errigal to let Wanama know it was safe.

"You just never know who's lurking around and who's really on your side," he declared. Wanama agreed and was grateful he'd taken such precautions. However she was confused as to how he knew exactly what was happening on the other side of the mountain.

"My friends on the other side were so keen to do something to help destroy that, that..." unable to think of a word which could suitably express his venom for Jezebel, he paused then shrieked "woman!" at the top of his voice.

Mel raised her eyebrows and looked at Wanama, who was clearly trying to remain serious while watching the weeman stamp his feet on the ground in annoyance at the thought of Jezebel. It was like he was performing a little ritual which no-one dared interrupt until he'd fully calmed down.

"Anyway," he continued. "I sent a message to them, my friends, to keep a watchful eye on you Mel, to make sure you were safe during your journey. Well, that was fine, until you went and disappeared!"

Mel felt like she was back in school. Chewing her bottom lip which she often did when feeling nervous, she screwed up her face and quietly whimpered, "Sorry. It's just that I fell down a deep pit and..." but she wasn't allowed to finish.

"I know that now, of course!"

He was becoming agitated and Wanama didn't know if she could bear to watch the whole 'over-excited' thing again.

He raised his head, sensing the depth of silent respect from the others. However, this was short-lived. Without warning, he quickly spun round and blurted out at tremendous speed, "Got to go. Can't wait around chattering. Time's running out. Wait for me at your house, Wanama." And with that, he disappeared out of sight, his voice trailing off into the distance.

"What a strange little man!" Mel was utterly astonished by what she'd just witnessed.

"Yes, but you know what?" continued Wanama. "Odd as it seems, he always turns up just at the right moment."

Shaking her head, Mel agreed.

Mel didn't stop talking the whole way down the mountain. Wanama tried to butt in a few times, but Mel just kept telling her about everything she had encountered during the last few days, without drawing breath.

Then there was Zurin.

"I don't know where he is now. She looked at Wanama, searching desperately for some kind of response which would make her feel better, but she was simply met with a silent nod.

"Come on now. I know it's hard for you, but we need to get back for The Blue Stone. Let's keep focused on that for the time-being."

There was much confusion among the antelope and ants. Not long after the attack had been called off, they were met by a horde of people led by Groggin.

"Help us!" cried Groggin. "For heaven's sake help us. Wanama has been tricked! Jezebel is up at Fire Rock waiting for her messenger to bring The Stone to her. Once she gets The Stone we're all doomed. She knows some of us have been working against her and I dread to think what she'll do to us and our families. Dear God, what are we going to do?"

The ants circled around the antelope and for the first time in their lives there seemed to be complete disorder.

"What does this mean?" asked the Queen Ant, expecting an intelligent explanation from her friends.

"Something's terribly wrong." Brazier shook his head, unable to grasp what was going on. "Our message was clear from Wanama. Her instructions were to call off the attack. Why would she tell us to do that if she hadn't got The Stone? Why on earth would she say that? I don't understand."

Searching for an answer, he lifted his head, and faced the others. Slowly, the grim reality of what had happened began to dawn on him. Surely not, it was inconceivable to think that someone on Wanama's side was working against her.

The atmosphere suddenly became thick and heavy. It was now clear to everyone that Wanama had been tricked into thinking The Blue Stone was back in safe hands. Only someone Wanama trusted could have convinced her of this.

Chapter 17

The weeman couldn't believe he'd got away with it! Fooling Wanama had been easier than he'd anticipated. Now that his job on this side of Errigal was complete, it was time to cross over to the dark side of the mountain where Jezebel would reward him for his good work. He sniggered to himself as he pondered on how Wanama would feel when she found out she'd been taken for a ride!

"Trust no-one," he mimicked. "You never know who's lurking around!"

He hadn't planned on becoming a traitor to Wanama... it just kind of happened.

Sebastian, the Jebelite living on Wanama's side of the mountain, had appeared out of no where and had been so persuasive.

"We need your help!" he pleaded. "Jezebel needs to get The Blue Stone before midnight. Don't let Wanama near The Stone. She doesn't know how to handle its power."

Now he was confused. Wanama had always seemed so smart.

"You must get The Stone from Mel. Go to the top of Errigal and wait for her. That way she'll have to call off the attack. You must understand. It would be disaster if Jezebel didn't gain power over Errigal. And another thing... she's promised to reward you greatly if you obey her orders. You will be given a position of authority in her Kingdom."

Sebastian went on to explain to the weeman how, once

he had managed to convince Wanama The Stone was safe, then he would have to leave this side of Errigal and step over the summit onto Jezebel's side.

"Make your way to Fire Rock where Jezebel will be waiting." He could see the weeman looked unsure about what to do.

"Listen, I've lived on the other side," he continued. "I promise you, it's so much more exciting than what you have here. People are rewarded for good work and get positions of power. Jezebel is the leader Errigal needs."

The weeman thought about the possibility of holding an important position and at the same time helping the people of Errigal.

"Wanama has no idea how to control the mountain. It would be so much better for the people of Errigal to be ruled by someone like Jezebel. Wanama could never compete with her strength."

As Sebastian spoke, the weeman reflected on how he had obediently followed Wanama's mother's instructions and really what thanks had he got? Certainly no position of authority had been offered. A new life, people looking up to him, with respect – this all suddenly seemed very attractive! The idea began to excite him. Perhaps this was his destiny. He had always been sure he was made for greater things. It's just that people never recognised it. Well, not until now. It didn't take much longer for him to come up with an answer.

"Okay, I'll do it!"

Everything had gone to plan. Now he was on his way

to join the Jebelites to help Jezebel gain full control of the mountain.

He had taken a disused dirt track which led him around the mountain, so he could make his journey over the summit without being seen.

Giving The Stone a gentle squeeze, he smiled. There was no sign of remorse or sadness as he stepped out of the light for the very last time into the dark shadows of Errigal.

Sebastian watched from afar, wishing he could accompany the weeman and join his friends on the other side. But that was not possible. Not anymore. Not now that he'd crossed over to Wanama's side of the mountain. He had to accept he could never live among the Jebelites again. Now that he was here, the most important thing for Sebastian was to make sure he didn't blow his cover. Convincing Wanama's people that he was one of them meant he could continue his undercover work for Jezebel. Someday it would all be worth it. In the meantime Sebastian had to remain discreet. So as soon as the weeman disappeared out of sight he slid into the woods to a place where he couldn't be found.

The river was filled with fish swimming at full pelt downstream leaping through the air to gain ground. They couldn't move quickly enough. Birds soared above, skimming across treetops,the meerkats wove through the forest racing to get to Wanama to let her know about the twist of events. News about The Blue Stone had just reached them and they knew they had to get to her before it was too late.

As the river took a sudden turn, the fish came to an abrupt halt. They didn't have to look too far, for there were Wanama and Mel standing at the river's edge, alerted by the sound coming from the mass movement within the river.

"What's up?" The look of fear was written all over Wanama's face.

"Jezebel used one of her messengers to trick you. The Blue Stone is being delivered to her now as we speak."

Wanama placed her hand over her mouth to stop herself from losing control.

"What?" spluttered Mel in disbelief. "How?"

Mel glanced up at Wanama who was staring straight ahead, numb from what she had just heard.

"The weeman?" cried Mel, her eyes wide in disbelief.

Not far behind the fish were the other animals who had been trying to help Wanama. No-one could disguise their total shock at what had just been revealed. The weeman becoming a traitor meant Jezebel already had some control on Wanama's side of the mountain. The thought of Jezebel becoming their new ruler was unthinkable! In despair, Wanama turned and made her way to her house. No-one dared to follow her. They all understood that right now, she needed to be alone.

Mel knew all they could do now was to wait. It would only be a matter of time before Jezebel's power would take over the whole of the mountain and beyond. The light would disappear and soon darkness would reign over both sides of Errigal.

Clambering over loose stones, the weeman eventually made it safely to the murky lake. Sebastian had given him careful instructions how to get to Fire Rock where Jezebel would be waiting. Perching himself on a rock, he rested a moment before continuing, but he had hardly drawn breath before he could hear shuffling from behind.

He jumped to his feet but wasn't quick enough. Caught in an arm lock he couldn't move his head.

"Where is she?" the person yelled into his ear.

"Where's who?"

"Jezebel, you fool!"

"Who is this? Let me go!" The weeman was starting to panic. He had only just arrived on Jezebel's side of the mountain and here he was in the tight grip of someone he didn't know.

"Who are you?" he screeched.

"Not a Jebelite that's all you need to know," came Zurin's sharp reply. He grabbed the weeman's wrist and with one sharp twist forced him to release The Stone.

Chapter 18

The antelope were ready for what happened next. Zurin had told them to wait under the trees which surrounded the lake, until he gave them the sign to advance. He reckoned the bats would be nearby, so he had to be careful. He would give a high pitched whistle to indicate he was ready. Brazier had instructed the others to move silently, which luckily came easily to them as they were so nimble. All were ready and waiting.

Suddenly the sky darkened. An icy wind swept through the trees. Brazier and his troupe held their ground, waiting for the sign. The branches above were swaying gently. After several moments Brazier looked up and was stunned to see the tops of the trees now rocking violently from side to side. Next, the dirt beneath them swirled around with such force that they had to close their eyes for protection. The heavens opened and sheets of rain poured down so rapidly, it nearly knocked Zurin and the weeman over.

Next came the hailstones. It was like being pelted with hundreds of gobstoppers! Each of them had to shield their face as the hail smacked against them. Never before had they experienced anything like it. The clouds swirled around in the night sky. Then, without warning, the wind swept through the trees and across the lake, throwing Zurin and the weeman to the ground. Attempting to get to their feet, both were hurled back down again. The sound of the gale was now deafening as it howled across the lake. The antelope remained under the trees, but Brazier was afraid that the strength of the wind was going to uproot everything around them.

Zurin knew he had to do something fast, otherwise the weeman would get away and Jezebel would be onto them. Twisting his arm up his back, Zurin gave the whistle. It was difficult to know if the antelope could hear him through the blasting wind and rain. His ears were pounding and Zurin didn't know how much longer he could keep this up. But as always they could be depended upon, even in the most severe of conditions.

With Brazier leading in front, forcing his way through the elements, the others followed until they finally reached Zurin.

"Thank goodness!" he gasped. "I was beginning to think you'd never make it. We're going to have to move quickly now if we want to get The Stone back to Wanama before Jezebel finds out."

He had managed to wrap it safely in a hanky and placed it carefully in his trouser pocket. Now all they needed to do was get to the top of Errigal and deliver The Stone back to its rightful owner. Zurin tightened his grip around the weeman's arm who was now screaming at the top of his voice, "Let me go! You'll never get away with this! She'll be onto you before you know it!"

Darkness was growing and a huge mist began to cover the lake. It was going to be even harder to get back up to the summit. Zurin turned to the weeman in desperation.

"Help us get The Stone back to Wanama and you'll be released. Try anything clever and you'll pay the consequences! Understood?"

Zurin lifted his head up by the hair and looking at him, waited for his reply.

"Well?"

Forcing a smile, the weeman stared straight at Zurin, then spat in his face! Zurin threw him back onto the ground. Wiping his face, he sighed.

"Let's move. We're going to have to rely on our instincts."

Led by Brazier, they battled their way through the elements, the other antelope surrounding the two men as they walked, helping provide some kind of protection.

Waiting in the treetops were Jezebel's messengers.

The bats had been instructed to guide the weeman to Jezebel, making sure no-one could get near him until The Stone was safely brought back.

However, they hadn't reckoned on the storm. The sound of the wind and the rain had made it impossible for them to locate the weeman, so they remained in the trees waiting for the storm to calm down. Eventually a gentle movement through the forest indicated the worst of the storm was over and swooping down from the trees, they flew out of the forest, towards the lake, certain they would find the weeman waiting for them as planned. But nothing! He'd vanished.

They continued their search for a few more minutes then panic set in. Things had gone horribly wrong. Surely he wouldn't have been stupid enough to disappear with The Stone. Jezebel would have to be told and they knew full well that she was not going to be pleased! Racing through the black sky, their wings beating rapidly, they flew in the direction of Fire Rock. There she was, standing waiting with a face on her like thunder.

"Where is he?"

"He's disappeared."

"What?" she shrieked.

"We did as you said. We waited in the trees until the handover, but the torrential rain and wind meant we couldn't hear a thing. By the time we flew out he'd gone."

"What are you talking about, you fools? What rain? What wind?"

The bats hesitated for a moment.

"M'am, we were caught in the storm. It was so harsh. It would've been suicide to fly in such conditions."

"There was no storm!" She paused for a moment, confident her messengers wouldn't be so dumb as to lie to her. She screwed up her eyes as the reality of what had happened began to dawn on her.

"We have forces working against us. The storm has been used as a way to get The Stone back to Wanama. Quick! We need to leave now. We must get to them before they reach the top of Errigal!"

Chapter 19

Mel couldn't remember a time in her life when she'd felt more alone. While everything around her looked so alive and vibrant glistening in the heat of the sun, here she was feeling like this was her darkest moment. Was Wanama ever going to come out of her house?

Reluctantly, she stood up and walked over to the edge of the river. Normally the beauty of the sparkling fish skimming between the rocks would have brought a smile to her face. Not now. If only they could tell her how to get out of this mess. If only they had the power to stop Jezebel from destroying everything that was good.

"Mel!"

Startled, she looked round.

"Come quick! Look over here. Something weird's happening."

Theo, one of the meerkats was scampering towards her.

She followed him until she could see what he was going on about. In front of her, huge rocks were tumbling towards the river. Everything was vibrating and Mel was sure she was experiencing an earth tremor. Without warning, the ground erupted and thousands of ants poured out, right in front of her eyes.

When the last couple finally emerged, the Queen Ant moved forward.

"Don't be afraid," she said, reassuring them that their mission was to help.

"You need to get to the top of Errigal as quickly as

possible. The Stone is on its way back to you as we speak."

"What?" exclaimed Mel in total disbelief. "How?"

"No time for questions. You've got to act with speed. Go and get Wanama, now! We've about twenty minutes before Sirius appears."

Without hesitation, Mel raced down to Wanama's house to find her standing on the porch. She had been drawn outside by all the commotion. She'd heard everything. Mel started to speak but Wanama didn't give her a chance.

"I know. Come on. Let's go. This time we're not going to let anything stop us getting it back."

As the sunlight spilled out onto the ground it seemed to map out a path for the two of them to follow. They continued as quickly as they could, without exchanging a single word.

Sam had not reckoned on this. She had made her way to Fire Rock, expecting to see Jezebel and the weeman. Her hopes were crushed when Jezebel told her what had happened.

"Follow me! They'll never get away with this."

"Wait!" Sam was tugging at her arm. "What about Sebastian? I could go over to the other side and let him know we need his help."

"No you idiot! He's in hiding – we'd never find him in time. No, keep moving. We need to get to the top of Errigal as fast as we can."

They were gaining good ground. Jezebel knew every part of the mountain, all the little shortcuts, even through the misty darkness.

"They'll not get the better of me," she snarled, spitting out the words.

In the distance they could hear movement. Something was ahead. The bats had flown on in front of Jezebel and Sam, but had just done a turnaround and were now heading back towards them. One of them called out as they swooped down.

"They're waiting at the top. We've got them."

Leaping ahead, Jezebel took a sharp left which gave her an advantage. Letting out a piercing whistle, she alerted her underground friends as backup. Instantly, a group of grotesque figures appeared by her side.

"To the top of Errigal, now! Stop the handover of The Stone! Go!"

Obediently they followed her instructions. With their long limbs, the under-grounders could outrun anything and Jezebel was relying on their speed. They were on their trail, so close, careful not to be heard.

Finally, turning to Sam, a sneering smile appeared over Jezebel's face.

"I'll take Wanama and you, my dear can have Mel!"

Sam smiled back, her heart racing with excitement at the prospect of getting even with this girl who had destroyed her credibility in front of her friends and Jezebel. Her hunger to share power with Jezebel was now stronger than ever.

Unaware of what was going on behind him, Zurin and Brazier continued to lead the weeman and the antelope towards the summit. Draped over the back of one of the antelope, the weeman hadn't stopped yelling since they'd left the lake.

Every few minutes Zurin checked to make sure The Stone was still safe in his pocket. He couldn't help thinking about how relieved Mel was going to be when she realised he had it. However, his thoughts were soon interrupted by a chorus of shrieks and flapping wings above. Zurin's heart sank as he raised his head and looked up to see a blanket of black descending upon them.

As their pace quickened, chaos set in.

"Run for cover!" Attempting to get everyone to safety, Brazier got behind the antelope, pushing them forward with his antlers. They ran in all directions, but even though these agile creatures could move like the wind, some just weren't fast enough. The bats quickly surrounded them and within seconds, one by one the antelope fell to their knees as they were viciously beaten by the smacking of the bats' wings. Twisting in pain, several of them fought back, kicking out with their hind legs in self defence, but the speed of the bats proved too much for them. Once the antelope were down, the little demons opened their wizened mouths, revealing sharp, chiselled teeth. They were trapped. Showing no mercy, the bats dug their teeth into the legs of each of the animals, causing overwhelming pain. Zurin, who was hiding behind a rock, could hear their whines which turned to muffles, then silence. His heart was thumping so hard he could hardly breathe. He looked around to try to find the weeman but he was gone. What next? How was he going to ensure Wanama got The Stone before it was too late?

A hand on his shoulder alerted him.

"Don't be frightened," the stranger whispered.

Zurin froze.

"Stay close to me. I'll lead you to the summit without Jezebel seeing us," he continued.

Zurin was desperate to turn around but the stranger quickly prodded him in the back as a signal to move forward.

"Keep your head down and try not to make a sound. The bats can hear everything."

Zurin moved obediently through the forest, as silently as he possibly could. His heart raced as he wondered if this person was genuinely trying to help him or was this one of the Jebelites trying to trick him.

"Keep going, we're nearly there."

Through the darkness Zurin could see an opening in the trees. Curious to find out who this person was, he waited until they reached the clearing then swung round to take a good look at him. At first all he could make out was nothing more than a small scrawny shape. Then Zurin grabbed him, drawing him towards his face for a clearer view.

"What?" He couldn't believe his eyes. "Matthieu!" Zurin could barely speak. This was too much to take in. He had almost given up hope of ever seeing his son again. Shaking his head, he reached out and placed a hand on his bony little shoulder. He swallowed hard as he tried to hold back the tears.

"Come here," he whispered.

Matthieu wrapped his arms around his dad's waist,

burying his head into his stomach.

A few moments passed then Matthieu looked up at his dad.

"I didn't think I'd ever see you again."

"I'm sorry, son. I'm so, so, sorry..." His voice trailed off.

"Matthieu, tell me," he asked, his voice suddenly changing. "Where's Mum?"

"Don't worry, she's ok, Dad. I've been keeping a close eye on her, though she doesn't know it. You see, she doesn't know where I am. Ever since you disappeared, I've been on the run."

"You're kidding! What did Jezebel do to you?" Zurin could feel the anger burning inside him.

"No Dad. It was my choice. After watching what she did to you, I promised myself I'd help to bring her down, whatever it took."

Zurin's admiration for his son was tinged with anger at his stupidity.

"You must be mad, Matthieu. If she'd found you she'd have killed you. Do you realise how much you've put yourself at risk?"

"I know, but I've kept myself well hidden from her. I've discovered all the best hiding places. Because I'm small it's been pretty easy." Matthieu stopped suddenly.

"We're going to have to move. I can hear voices. They'll have this place surrounded in no time. Come on. I know a short-cut to the top."

Zurin stopped himself from saying anymore for now. He didn't allow himself to think about how his son had been able to survive alone, out in the wild and how his mother must be out of her mind with worry. Looking at him he felt choked. Matthieu looked half starved, a mere shadow of what he used to be.

He watched how his son managed to dart to and fro between the rocks and bushes. He seemed to know every twist and turn along the way.

"Not much further now." Matthieu's eyes darted around as he crept forward, ensuring there were no imminent signs of danger.

"Look!" he gasped pointing ahead.

In the distance, at the top of the mountain, Zurin could see two small figures standing swathed in sunlight amidst all the darkness.

"Wait here Matthieu. Don't move. I'll be back in a minute." Climbing up a little further he waved his arms in an attempt to get Mel's attention.

"Zurin, is that you?" Waving frantically she watched as her friend came into sight.

"I thought you were dead," she whispered.

He was running now, astounded at the speed at which he could move.

"That's it!" yelled Mel. "Keep going Zurin, you're nearly there."

His little legs couldn't go any faster as he clambered over the stony ground, but the thought of handing over this precious stone was enough encouragement for him. It was a tough climb and he'd just about made it.

"Zurin, look out!" Wanama noticed several dark figures emerging from the trees, moving in his direction.

He spun round just in time to catch a glimpse of

something several feet behind. It was the under-grounders. Running on, he tried to shake them off, but it was proving impossible. Others appeared in front and from the sides. He was surrounded. As they moved closer, Zurin soon realised that this was the same group of people who had captured him before. Their freakish features made them easy to identify.

Mel and Wanama looked at each other. How could they help Zurin? Time was running out. They had to do something fast! Wanama caught Mel's eyes and held her look for a moment. Instinctively, Mel knew what Wanama was thinking – only one of them could step over into Jezebel's world.

"Wait for me, Wanama." Mel whispered the words, forcing herself to be brave.

Before Wanama had a chance to speak, Mel had already taken to her heels and was running towards Zurin, who was now trapped. He wrapped his fingers tightly around The Stone, hoping for extra strength and wisdom as to what to do, watching with terror as the under-grounders closed in on him. He didn't dare look around to see if Matthieu was ok. He couldn't risk blowing his cover.

"Hey! Over here!" A shout made each one of them turn round in surprise.

"You've the wrong person! If it's The Stone you want here, take it. Let Zurin go and I'll give it to you. He's worth more to me than a stupid stone." Mel spoke with a confidence which surprised even her.

The men looked at one another, confused by the sudden turn of events.

Stepping away from Zurin, one of them turned towards Mel,

"How do we know you've got it? Prove it!"

"You'll just have to trust me," came back the reply. "Release Zurin first and I'll show it to you." She waited, but could see they were unsure about what to do.

"Think about it," she continued. "You'll be heroes in Jezebel's eyes. Just imagine how you'll be rewarded. I wouldn't think you'd be condemned any longer to a life underground."

Mel paused to let them reflect on what she'd just said. Her heart was racing and she didn't dare look up at Wanama who was waiting at the top.

After some muttering, one of the group spoke. "Ok. We'll let Zurin go. But you must come down to us with The Stone. And don't try anything clever!" Some of the other under-grounders were looking over their shoulders in the hope of Jezebel and Sam appearing, not so sure that this was a good idea.

Terrified at the prospect of things going horribly wrong, Mel began her descent. Although it wasn't very far, every step felt like a mile. When she was within a few feet of the group she addressed them.

"Let him go, I'm going nowhere."

"We want to see The Stone!"

"Not till you let him go. You can't fool me!"

Mel clenched her fists, trying to remain calm. She wasn't sure how long she could keep this up.

"Do as she says." A familiar voice could be heard from the trees. It was Sam. She'd been waiting in the background, ready to move in when the time was right.

"I'll take over from here. Jezebel will be told of the good work you've done."

The men bowed their heads and complied with Sam's request.

Sam realised this was now her big chance to impress her leader.

They stepped aside and allowed Zurin to walk free. He turned to Mel who was face to face with Sam. Nervously, he slipped his hand in his pocket. Yes, it was still there. Without flinching, he walked on, eyes fixed firmly on the bright light ahead. He moved faster, knowing that it would only be moments before Mel's clever plan would be uncovered.

"So Mel, we meet again." Although Sam's tone terrified her, she tried to remain calm, giving Zurin as much time as possible to make it to Wanama. For how much longer she could delay the inevitable, she didn't know. Then, without warning, Sam grabbed Mel by the hair, making her demand.

"Where is it? Hand it over, you little runt!"

Sam kept yanking her hair until she knew she couldn't hold back any longer.

"I haven't got it."

In a panic, Sam threw her to the ground.

She couldn't contain her anger.

"You don't know what you've done, you little fool!"

Screeching at the top of her voice, she tried to get the attention of the under-grounders who were now on their way back home.

"Get back over here!" she yelled.

Straight away, the group stopped in their tracks. Then, without further hesitation, took to their heels in the direction of Zurin.

"Get him!" The shouts were loud and clear.

That was it. They knew. Increasing his speed, Zurin looked up and was so close he could see Wanama's face. Reaching out her hands in a final attempt to retrieve The Stone, she pleaded,

"Throw it Zurin. It's our last chance!"

Reaching deep into his pocket, he grabbed The Stone and lifting it out, tossed it high up into the sky towards Wanama. For a moment, everyone held their breath as it spun around, getting higher and higher up into the atmosphere. Waiting for it to fall back down again felt like an eternity. Wanama stood transfixed, hands outstretched, ready to catch it on its descent.

"Come on," she muttered to herself. "Fall on this side of the mountain."

Her hands were now shaking and her body felt weak at the thought of The Stone disappearing out of sight for ever.

To everyone's amazement, the sky blackened and an eerie silence filled the air. No-one dared to move, all wondering what was going to happen next. Amidst the darkness Wanama could detect a tiny light in the distance.

"There it is," she announced, pointing in its direction.

It was like a satellite moving with such force and speed, higher and higher, up into the atmosphere. Then with the same suddenness with which it appeared, it halted. No-one moved a muscle. Not a single sound could be heard as everything became perfectly still.

Chapter 20

Jezebel appeared out from the trees where she had been hiding and was now standing only a few feet from Wanama who was on the other side of the summit. Neither one looked at the other, only able to stare upwards at the tiny light circling in the sky above them.

A sudden flash from the light startled everyone and acted as a warning that something was about to happen. Not a single sound could be heard. Then – Boom! The force of the explosion threw everyone to the ground. Mel was sure the whole sky had exploded right above them. Covering her ears, which were now ringing from the impact of the sound, she looked upwards to find the sky filled with a multitude of colours flashing to and fro.

Stepping forward, Wanama gasped at the spectacle before her. She had never seen anything like it. But quickly her thoughts turned to The Stone. Where was it?

Circling around for a few more minutes, The Stone, which was now a blinding core of light, began to fall. The speed at which it descended was incredible! Poised at the summit, both women continued to stare as it plummeted through the air. It was difficult to tell on which side of the mountain it was going to land, but they were both ready to catch it. The Stone bolted down at a furious rate, stopping at tree level, right above the two women. Jezebel reached first, but being the smaller, it was just too high for her. Raising her arm, Wanama reached up towards The Stone and, with a magnetic force, it gently fell into the palm of her hand. She held it tightly, breathing a sigh of relief. Finally she'd got it back.

"You'll never win this battle!"

Wanama recognised the voice straight away, as she turned towards Jezebel.

"The Stone was left to me," said Wanama in a controlled tone, "and you know it!"

Jezebel looked straight at her.

"What kind of leader are you anyway? You're nothing! You're a disgrace – Errigal needs someone strong, one who takes command."

Wanama was alarmed by the depth of hatred she saw in Jezebel's eyes. She couldn't help thinking about her mother's final message, warning her of the disorder which would occur if The Stone ever got into Jezebel's hands. If nothing else, she owed it to her mother to keep her wish.

"Leave us in peace, Jezebel. Go back to your people where you belong. I don't want to fight with you anymore. The Blue Stone was left to me and I don't ever intend to let it go. You know that I'll do whatever it takes to make sure it never gets into the wrong hands again."

Jezebel stepped closer."Even if it means destroying Mel?"

"What are you talking about? Mel means nothing to you now! Let her go!"

Wanama glared at her, then glanced at Mel. Sam had her arm so tightly around Mel's neck she could hardly breathe.

"Let's look on this as a kind of, let me see, hmm, yes a

kind of ransom. Now you see, my dear Wanama, you do have a choice. You give me The Stone and you get Mel back. It's quite simple, really."

Suddenly Wanama broke down, losing control of her emotions.

"You are cruel beyond words!" she cried.

Knowing that it wasn't long now before Sirius appeared above Errigal, Wanama felt beaten. She fell to her knees.

"Ok, Sam squeeze tighter," instructed Jezebel. Sam did as she was told and gasps could be heard from Mel as she started to feel light-headed.

"Well, my dear, what's it to be?"

The tension was unbearable, everyone anxious for Wanama to make her decision before it was too late.

A sudden noise from the forest changed everything. It was Brazier. Stepping out into the clearing he marked his target by pointing his antlers towards Sam. Then, lowering his head, he charged. It all happened so fast no-one knew what to do. Skidding to a halt in front of Sam, he twisted on his hooves, turning his back against her. Sam was terrified at the size of the beast, so close to her. She tried to make her escape, but Brazier was too quick. Lifting his hind legs he kicked her, causing her to fall to the ground. As she fell, Brazier managed to shuffle Mel out of her reach.

"Run for your life!" he yelled.

"What about you?" shouted Mel who was now running towards Wanama.

"Don't worry about me, just keep going!"

Yells could be heard from Jezebel instructing her

helpers to chase Mel. The bats were fighting to get to her, but try as they might, they just couldn't manage it.

As Mel approached the summit you could see a strange glow surrounding her. The light carried her straight to Wanama.

"You're safe, Mel," she whispered, overcome with the joy she felt as Mel collapsed like a child into her arms. "Your job's done."

Chapter 21

It was nearly time. The sky was completely clear.

"Any moment now we'll see Sirius."

This was what Wanama had been waiting for. Soon the light from Sirius would change everything. The power in The Blue Stone would be released at last and she would be given the power to rule over Errigal.

"I can't believe it. It's finally happening!"

But Mel wasn't listening. She was more concerned about her friends on the other side of the mountain. What would become of Zurin and Groggin and all those other families? There were so many innocent lives to consider.

A light began to appear in the distance. Wanama could just about make it out. Gradually it became brighter and brighter until after several minutes, the whole sky was lit up.

"Look Mel! Isn't it amazing?"

The light from Sirius streamed down onto Errigal like a pathway from heaven. Wanama started to walk in its direction, ready to unfold her hand to reveal The Blue Stone.

Mel looked on, numbed by everything that had happened. She missed her friends so much that her heart ached to see them again. "Over here!" summoned Wanama. "What you're about to witness only happens once in a lifetime."

Mel walked over and was soon encased in blinding light.

"What's happening?"

"Isn't it wonderful?" said Wanama, stunned by the whole experience.

Even though Mel couldn't see her friend, she could hear the joy in her voice. She knew they were now safe from the threat of Jezebel.

With both arms outstretched, Wanama held The Blue Stone high above her head. She held it there for a few moments, allowing the light from Sirius to surround it.

"It's like electricity going through my body!" Wanama couldn't contain her excitement. "It's really happening! I can feel the power through every bone. Incredible!"

Mel reached out her hand and gently touched her friend to let her know she was right there. Wanama was now in some kind of trance, inviting the light to touch every part of her. She was spinning, arms high above her head chanting words which Mel couldn't understand.

Then suddenly, all the light from the star poured onto Wanama, circling around her at great speed, its intensity so powerful Mel was forced to turn away. Wanama fell to her knees as Mel covered her face with her hands, blinded by the startling brightness surrounding them.

Finally, the brilliance of Sirius began to fade and the largest star in the sky gradually transformed into a tiny insignificant dot, taking its place among the millions of others in the universe.

"Unbelievable!" murmured Wanama as she emerged from her trance.

"Wow! That was simply amazing." Shaking her head in disbelief she continued, "It's done Mel. The power's been released. I'm the ruler over Errigal. It's only a matter of time now before Jezebel's power weakens and mine becomes stronger. It's because of you that this has been possible."

Mel smiled but her expression quickly changed as her thoughts turned to her friends on the other side of the mountain.

"What now? Can we get Zurin and the others safely over to this side away from that beast?"

Wanama knew this wasn't going to be easy, but she owed it to Mel to tell her the truth.

"Listen to me. There's something you need to know." She took a deep breath.

"Your friends, Zurin and Groggin, well they're not exactly strangers to me."

Mel looked at Wanama suspiciously, not sure she wanted to hear what was coming next.

"I know this is going to come as a bit of a shock, but you see their families used to live on this side of the mountain."

Mel's expression suddenly changed to total disbelief.

"Unfortunately a couple of Jebelites stepped over the summit from the dark side. Their mission was to steal the Blue Stone for Jezebel. However, their plan failed and one of them fell to his death in the process. Furious, the other Jebelite who was left, decided to take revenge. He cunningly lured all the children from here to the top of the mountain. Once they were at the top, they were forced over to the other side with no return and used to work for Jezebel. Her hopes were to expand her Kingdom so that one day she would have complete control of Errigal. As the children were forced across the summit, their screams could be heard for miles. Parents immediately stopped what they were doing and ran to their rescue, desperate to find out what was going on. Unfortunately most of them were too late. All they could do was stand and listen to the helpless cries from their children as they were dragged down the other side of the mountain."

Mel couldn't believe what she was hearing.

"But some simply couldn't bear to think of their loved ones being led into that unknown world of darkness. The first one to take a step across was Groggin, followed by Zurin. Next their wives and before we knew it everyone had stepped over to the other side, leaving only me." She hung her head in despair. "Somebody had to stay."

Mel was beginning to understand the significance of what she was being told.

"And once they took a step across, that was it. No return. Is that what you're saying?"

"That's what I'm saying. I'm sorry Mel. Much as I'd love to be able to bring these people back, I can't. They chose to cross the summit knowing they could never return. But listen. In time, Jezebel's power will gradually diminish and mine will get stronger. I will eventually have complete control of the other side of Errigal."

"But it's going to be too late for Zurin and Groggin! We need to do something now!" She was pleading with Wanama. "We can't stand here knowing they'll be punished for helping us."

For a few moments, no words were exchanged. Mel couldn't bear to look at Wanama for fear she would break down. Wanama, however, could do nothing but stare longingly at this young girl, trying desperately to make sense of what she was saying.

Finally Mel broke the silence.

"They're my friends. I can't just abandon them, knowing they sacrificed everything to help us."

"Look, you have to understand, there's nothing more you can do for them. Helping us stop Jezebel having control of The Blue Stone is as much as they could have hoped for. Their comfort will be in the knowledge that she'll never have control of the mountain."

Mel felt defeated. She glanced at Wanama who was now holding her hand out as a sign for her to follow. Walking towards her, Mel didn't utter another word. She locked her arm in Wanama's and slowly both began their descent.

The air grew warmer and everything became brighter. Mel looked closely at the trees surrounding them which were covered in new leaves. The stream glistened as it twisted down over the rocks leading the way back to Wanama's home.

As word quickly spread about how Wanama had become empowered by The Blue Stone, one by one the animals started to emerge from the woodland, wanting to show their gratitude. The knowledge that she now was their true leader was indeed cause for great celebration.

Fish began leaping and somersaulting in the air, ecstatic at the news they'd just heard. Birds of all shapes and sizes appeared in multitudes overhead, swooping and circling above, frantically flapping their wings as they applauded their leader. The warm, silent air had been welcomingly disturbed by the cheerful sound of every living creature on this side of the mountain. Wanama was speechless! As she looked around at all the faithful folk who had come out in support, her gaze fell upon a solitary figure huddled against a tree. He stood watching the display in disgust. Sebastian had done everything he could to make sure Jezebel gained power. He had worked tirelessly to try to get The Blue Stone to her. This was not how it was all supposed to end. Unable to watch anymore, he turned away and, feeling defeated, slipped back into the forest leaving the others to continue with their celebrations.

Smiling that warm, endearing smile which everyone loved, Wanama looked round and addressed her followers.

"Thank you, my dear friends, for believing in me. As you know, The Blue Stone of Errigal has now been returned to me and the power which has been locked inside it for hundreds of years has been released. I am honoured that I have been chosen to lead you all and I have been given the power to do so with the help of Sirius. The power I've been given is much stronger than any power Jezebel possesses. She can't touch us now."

Cheers and yells of support echoed throughout the mountain. Pausing through all the noise, Wanama looked around at the huge crowd which had gathered so quickly, then held her hands up indicating she had more to add.

"If I could just finish by saying, all of this couldn't have happened without the help of many of our friends on both this side and the other side of Errigal. However, one young girl risked her life to bring back The Blue Stone. Without her we would now all be under the dictatorship of Jezebel, living in total darkness. Because of Mel, life can continue on here without us having the worry of the threat of Jezebel taking over. You have my absolute word I will lead by example, working for the good of all the people on Errigal. Now, can we please show our appreciation for what Mel has done for us."

For a few moments there was silence. At first Wanama wasn't sure if the crowd was completely with her. Then, without warning, the whole place erupted into rapturous applause.

While this was happening, Wanama looked around to try to find her friend, keen to bring her up to the front, but it was too difficult. The place was filled with so many different creatures it was impossible to locate her.

Theo was standing in front of Wanama. Leaning over, she mouthed to him through all the cheering,

"Where is she?"

Looking around with his beady little eyes, he turned to face her. He looked so tiny beside her large frame. Gently, he took a deep breath.

"You know what? I think she's returned home."

Wanama hadn't wanted to admit it but she felt he was right. Mel had her own life to go back to, down in the village where she belonged. She couldn't have expected her to stay here on Errigal and it wasn't her style to be in the middle of all this praise and recognition. She knew her work was finished on Errigal and she wouldn't have been one for lengthy, emotional good-byes.

"You're right," she finally admitted. "But I'm so going to miss her."

"Come on," encouraged Theo.

Smiling at each other they walked down the mountain as the animals parted, clearing a pathway to allow them to make their exit.

Fortunately for Wanama she didn't know the truth.

Somewhere at the top of Errigal stood a young girl who hadn't been able to leave her friends. She had quietly broken away while Wanama had been talking to the crowd and had begun to climb back up the mountain until finally she had stopped in her tracks, taking a brief moment to look up at the crest of Errigal. Best that Wanama didn't know that during her speech, Mel had stepped over into the dark world, desperate to save her friends from Jezebel.

As she continued her descent, Wanama took comfort in the belief that Mel had been led back home safely by the mountain spirits. Inhaling the warm air, she felt refreshed as she closed her eyes to fully appreciate the moment. It was as if time had become frozen, just for an instant. Then, out of nowhere, a cool breeze brushed across Wanama's face as a stark reminder that nothing stays the same for long on Errigal...

About the Author

Born in Belfast, Colleen spent her early childhood in Vancouver and Seattle where her father worked as an engineer. Her family returned to live in East Belfast in 1969. She went on to train at Stranmillis College, Belfast and has worked as a primary school teacher for the last 20 years.

Errigal, Search for The Blue Stone is her first novel, inspired by childhood holidays spent in Bunbeg, Donegal where she climbed Mount Errigal as a young girl. She now lives in Holywood, County Down and is married to Trevor. They have three children, Emma, Hannah and Michael.